A DECLARATION OF LOVE

Daniel led Kate to where the chaise shielded them from the twins' view.

"I am tired of talking about Percy," he said. "Let's switch topics."

"To what?"

Daniel put his hands around Kate's waist and lowered his lips over hers in a gentle, non-invasive kiss.

Her hands went around his neck. His mouth was achingly sweet. Kate felt warm and pleasantly shivery in his embrace.

She kissed him back before he lifted his lips and looked down at her.

"There is a vast difference between real love and temporary infatuation," he said softly.

From *One True Love*, by Alice Holden

ON BENDED KNEE

Alice Holden

Kate Huntington

~~Laura Paquet~~

ZEBRA BOOKS
Kensington Publishing Corp.
http://www.kensingtonbooks.com

ZEBRA BOOKS are published by

Kensington Publishing Corp.
850 Third Avenue
New York, NY 10022

All Kensington titles, imprints and distributed lines are
available at special quantity discounts for bulk purchases for
sales promotion, premiums, fund-raising, educational or
institutional use.

Special book excerpts or customized printings can also be
created to fit specific needs. For details, write or phone the
office of the Kensington Special Sales Manager: Kensington
Publishing Corp., 850 Third Avenue, New York, NY 10022.
Attn. Special Sales Department. Phone: 1-800-221-2647.

Zebra and the Z logo Reg. U.S. Pat. & TM Off.

First Printing: June 2003
10 9 8 7 6 5 4 3 2 1

Printed in the United States of America

CONTENTS

ONE TRUE LOVE

Alice Holden

One

With the toe of her black half boot, Kate Hamilton tamped the loose soil around a pink petunia in the penny-sized garden beside the door to her grandparents' home in a former carriage house.

"There's Daniel Nealy," her grandmother said, squinting into the late afternoon sun. "He's Penny's doctor."

Kate pushed back her straw hat and ran a forearm over her damp forehead and watched the tall man stride across the lawn toward them. Looking austere in a black coat and trousers which were tucked into black workmanlike boots, his dark hair gleamed in the sunlight.

"So, he's the veterinarian," Kate said. She did not hide her interest as she pulled down her flat hat to shade her pale skin.

"Aye, girl." Cloris Franklin's voice emphasized the broad vowels of her humble origins. "He leased the cottage across the way when he came to work in the district some three years ago. A bachelor, he is. A widow woman from the village, Rosie Marr, by name, comes thrice a week to clean up for him."

Kate knew that the interjection that Mr. Nealy was a bachelor was deliberate. Her grandmother had not given up hope that Kate would be swept up into wedded bliss even at her advanced age of five-and-twenty. Kate herself was more realistic. She had had sparse social congress with eligible young men when she was right for receiving suitors, and it was a little late in the day now for romance.

Since strangers in the area were rare, Kate gave no weight to the veterinarian's unconcealed interest in her as he stepped from the freshly mown grass to the graveled drive. He was simply wondering who she was.

Kate bobbed her head slightly when her grandmother introduced her to Mr. Nealy. His smile was amiable, his deep brown eyes friendly.

"Your servant, Miss Hamilton," he said in a cultured accent that identified him, despite his occupation, as a member of the upper classes. He turned to speak to her grandmother.

"I brought you a salve that might help with the rash on your spaniel's legs, Mrs. Cloris," he said, using the conventional title of respect before her grandmother's given name.

"How kind of you, Daniel," Cloris said, taking the opaque jar from him. "I shall have my Joseph settle the reckoning with you next quarter day."

Mr. Nealy moved his large hand in a dismissing gesture. "No need, ma'am, it is a sample a tradesman gave me to try. We can see if the concoction works on Penny before I give the merchant my custom."

Kate studied Mr. Nealy while he and her grandmother discussed how to apply the salve to the dog's infection. She judged him to be about thirty. He had considerable height but was not of a burly girth. His chiseled visage was pleasantly respectable rather than outrightly handsome.

He turned unexpectedly toward Kate as she stared.

"For how long will you be visiting your grandparents, Miss Hamilton?" he asked.

Kate felt a rush of heat on her cheeks at being caught gawking. Averting her eyes to the pink and white petunias, she temporized, "For a time."

"Kate's father passed away recently, and she is going to live with us now," Cloris said, more precisely.

Mr. Nealy offered his condolences. Kate thanked him and went back to her gardening. She knelt down onto a knee pad and set another plant into the soft ground.

Just then, the window above their heads shot open and Joseph Franklin leaned his muscular arms on the sill. "What would you have me do with the pot of lamb stew, Clorry? It's boiling rather fiercely."

Cloris tilted her gray head back to look up at her husband. "Pull it off to the side away from the fire. I am coming right up."

Joseph vanished from the window.

Stripping her gardening gloves from her hands, Cloris tossed them into a wooden carrier at her feet and muttered, "You would think a grown man, even one who did not know his way around in the kitchen, could figure that out for himself."

Both Kate and Mr. Nealy smiled. Cloris smiled with them.

"Please finish up the planting for me, Katie dear," she said. "Farewell, Daniel."

As she departed through the ground-level door which opened to the stairs that led to the flat above, Joseph reappeared at the window and talked with Mr. Nealy.

Kate's grandfather was the longtime steward of the lakeside estate that was owned by the Marchands, an aristocratic family, who these days derived most of their income from investments rather than from the land.

Before her grandfather finally closed the window, Kate heard the two men discuss the health of the sheep and horses and the dairy cows that supplied milk for the main house and some of the lake cottages.

Mr. Nealy lingered while Kate planted the last petunia. She had been taking occasional sideways glances at him while he talked with Joseph. He was soft-spoken for such a big man and had a ready smile.

She stood up, gathered her tools into the wooden caddy, removed her work gloves, and added them to the box.

"Where was your home?" Mr. Nealy asked her, conversationally.

Kate crammed the clay pots in which the plants had

been started from seeds in the greenhouse during the winter into a wicker basket.

"London," she said. "The house was sold on my father's death. My mother died several years ago. I am here because Cloris and Joseph Franklin are the only family left to me."

Picking up the box of gardening tools, Kate carried it into one of the bays of the carriage house, where a barouche, a wagon, and a dogcart along with assorted farm equipment were stored.

Mr. Nealy picked up the wicker basket of clay pots and took it into the bays where years ago the vehicles of visitors to the main house where the Viscount Marchand and his wife and their eight-year-old twin daughters now dwelled during the summer had been parked.

He set the basket down where Kate indicated and stood beside a plow, running his hand over the wooden handle, which had been worn smooth by years of use.

"Pray forgive me, Miss Hamilton. I mean no disrespect, but you do not speak with the plain country accents of your grandparents. Yet your mother was their daughter, am I right?"

"Are you always so nosy on short acquaintance, Mr. Nealy?" she said, more amused than annoyed.

His brown eyes widened for a second, but then he chuckled. "Don't you know it is human nature to pry, Miss Hamilton? But you can send me away if I have offended you."

She looked at him for a long moment, not sure how to reply, but, of course, it would be rude to send him away, and he hadn't really offended her.

"My mother married above her station," she said, honestly. "My father was a noted archeologist, knighted for his discoveries, who made an adequate income for us to live a solid middle-class life. My mother died when I was seventeen. My father developed a bad heart shortly afterwards, and I took care of the house and helped him consolidate his research and write up reports since he could no longer go out in the field."

"And now?"

Kate shook the dirt from the apron she wore over an old brown dress and hung it on a nail.

"I have a small competence from the sale of the London house," she said, "but not enough to live on my own. I want to find a position as a governess, for I do not want to be a burden to my grandparents."

Kate walked toward the carriage house door. Mr. Nealy fell in step beside her.

"A governess," he repeated. He stopped suddenly. "Good gracious, Miss Hamilton, you may just have fallen into a bit of serendipity."

Kate walked back toward him. "How so?" she said, looking up into his bemused face.

"The Marchand twins' governess left unexpectedly last week. The viscount is looking for someone to look after his eight-year-old girls."

His words gained Kate's immediate attention. Could this indeed be a happy miracle?

Kate shook her head. "I have the education, but I have no experience working with children."

"Your age may work in your favor. The last governess was only eighteen. Addison, that is Lord Marchand, did say something about wanting someone older and better qualified, but I think he might be willing to hire you for the summer if your education is satisfactory. After all, he is in somewhat of a bind. He would have a devil of a time getting an experienced governess to come from London on such short notice."

"Oh," Kate moaned, "I don't know."

"Would you take the position if it was offered to you?" Mr. Nealy asked, stroking his strong chin.

"Of course," she said without hesitation. "I could stay near to my grandparents and get some much-needed experience. I would be a crackbrain not to."

"Then?" he said, raising his brow.

"I cannot just knock on the door and impudently put myself forth for a position which has not even been posted."

Mr. Nealy nodded his understanding. "I tell you what, I am expected at the main house for supper at six," he said. "I can feel Lord Marchand out for you."

"You would do that for me?" Kate was astonished. "But I cannot impose on you," she said, but she knew that her eyes spoke differently.

"I volunteered, Miss Hamilton," he said generously. "Lord Marchand is a longtime friend. We go way back."

She did not know what to say, except, "Thank you."

Kate changed into a clean cotton gown and came into the parlor from her bedroom. Joseph sat in a rocking chair near the fireplace, reading a week-old copy of the London *Times*, while Penny, the King Charles spaniel, napped on the hearth rug near his feet.

Her grandfather looked up and returned her smile before going back to his reading. Kate loved him dearly. Her summers here in the country had been the happiest times of her childhood.

Joseph had often taken her up before him on his horse when he rode over the estate and spoke to her about his duties. She learned the names of all the workers and met their families at a very young age. It was her grandfather who first taught her about the wildlife in and around the lake, the names of the fish and the birds.

Kate was bursting to discuss her conversation with Mr. Nealy with him, but she checked herself, for she knew that Joseph opposed her plans to live with a strange family in the City as a governess. Perhaps he would be supportive if the family were the Marchands, people he knew.

But Mr. Nealy might be one of those gentlemen who

promised much, but delivered nothing. Yet he did not strike her as being a blowhard.

Kate joined her grandmother in the kitchen, where the delicious aroma of lamb stew permeated the air.

Joseph maintained that Kate today looked like Cloris when he had married her. Kate's full-length mirror confirmed it. Like her grandmother, she was slender and a little taller than average for a woman. The rich brown streaks among Cloris's gray were the same shade of chestnut as Kate's own thick locks. And she had her grandmother's small nose and big brown eyes.

Cloris put a basket of bread on the table. "What were you and Daniel Nealy talking about?" she asked. "It was quite some time before he crossed the green back to his own place."

"Oh, this and that," Kate said noncommittally.

Her grandmother filled individual soup bowls at the iron stove with lamb stew and brought them back one at a time to the oak table, the surface of which showed the wear of forty-five years of daily use.

"Such a solid and sensible man," Cloris said. "Thirty and still not married. A real catch. Did you like him?"

Kate did not take the bait. "Grandpa, supper," she called and sat down at her usual place at the table.

Joseph said grace. The moment Cloris raised her bowed head, she went on lauding Mr. Nealy. "Daniel's father is Lord Thomas Nealy, a wealthy baron, Kate. His mother is the third daughter of an earl. He has a right to be high-and-mighty, but he isn't. Is he, Joseph?"

"Not in the least," her husband agreed. "Daniel is smart and no popinjay."

Kate could not help herself from asking, for she now, in truth, had a real interest in Mr. Nealy. "How came he to be a veterinarian, do you suppose?"

"Daniel is the youngest of three boys," Joseph said, "but Lord Nealy did right by all his sons, not just the heir. When Daniel chose his unusual occupation, the baron sent him at great expense to France for his veterinary studies." He paused, holding a soup spoon in the air. "Some fancy-sounding place."

"The École Nationale Vétérinaire in Lyons, perhaps," Kate suggested. She had heard the school was the best and oldest such institute founded around 1762, if her memory served.

"Aye, that is it," Joseph said. "Daniel Nealy has come to be highly regarded hereabouts these three years, not only as a skilled and well-educated animal doctor, but also as an honest and honorable man."

Daniel Nealy did not sound like a man who made empty promises, Kate thought.

Her deduction was justified later the same evening. Kate's heart raced as she passed Joseph, who had answered the door. He came up the stairs as she went down, his gray eyes filled with questions which she could not yet answer.

Mr. Nealy stood inside the door, out of the wind.

"Lord Marchand will interview you tomorrow at the main house at ten o'clock," he said.

Kate thanked Mr. Nealy over and over again.

He laughed, but seemed quite pleased.

"I would take you over to the main house myself and introduce you to the Marchands, but I have an appointment with a young cow whom I suspect is suffering from milk fever."

He opened the door. "Good luck," he said and walked off across the lawn to his own house.

Kate looked after him in wonder. No one outside of her family had ever intervened personally on her behalf before with a third party as Mr. Nealy had done. Somehow she felt that he was going to become a good friend.

Two

From the hilltop, Kate looked down at the fieldstone house that had been the country residence of the Earls of Keith since the early 1700s. The present earl, Viscount Marchand's father, had sold off parcels of the land around the lake when his estate had ceased to be profitable. Charming homes of a recent vintage now rimmed the shore, the newest built just four years ago.

Kate thought that she would be perfectly content to spend the rest of her life in a lake house. There was something so peaceful, idyllic, about the lake, surrounded by the thick, leafy woods. But unless she found a pot of gold at the end of the rainbow, that was never going to happen. Price and demand put the lake properties beyond the pocketbooks of all but the wealthiest buyers.

Kate lifted the floral enameled watch pinned to the lapel of her gray spencer and seeing that it was nearly ten o'clock, she hurried down the pebbled path to the front steps.

Suddenly, she was having second thoughts and a case of nerves. Whatever had possessed her to think that she could apply for a position as a governess without qualifications or experience? Taking heart from the cheerful yellow daffodils beside the porch, she mounted the stone steps to the solid oak door. But before she could reach for the brass knocker, the door flew open and a man nearly bowled her over.

He seized her shoulders and pulled her against his chest,

saving her from a nasty fall backward down the steep steps.

"Good Lord," he exclaimed. "Are you all right?"

Kate gazed into a pair of anxious blue eyes the color of a perfect summer sky and nodded, too breathless to speak. He had the face of an angel and was the handsomest man that Kate had ever seen.

He let her go and bent down and retrieved the curly brimmed hat which had somehow ended up on the porch.

"I am Lord Percy Wescott," he said, "Lord Marchand's brother-in-law. And, I know that you are Joseph the steward's granddaughter, but your name is . . . ?" His blond locks shown like gold in the morning sun.

"Katherine Hamilton," she said, her pounding heart beginning to still. "I am here to interview for the post of governess."

"This way," he said and backed through the door, which still stood open, beckoning with a waggle of an elegantly gloved finger. He was only an inch or so taller than Kate, but his body was perfectly proportioned for his height.

Kate followed him to a drawing room off the vestibule, where he invited her to sit down on a Sheraton sofa.

"I shall have you announced, Miss Hamilton," he said, courteously, and pulled the bellrope on the wall behind her before he sat down in a wing chair and stretched out his legs in front of him.

"Is Daniel Nealy a close friend?" he asked. "I understand from m'sister that he championed you for the job."

Kate's eyes widened. *"Championed* is a bit strong, my lord. Mr. Nealy and I met mere days ago when he brought some medicine for my grandmother's dog to the carriage house."

"That so," he said. He raised his brow.

"He is my grandparents' associate," she said, but left it at that, for the truth, if she chose to give it to him, would involve a needlessly lengthy explanation.

The young lord looked at her for a moment as if he expected her to say more, but at that moment the butler came to the door.

"Spakes, will you please inform his lordship that Miss Hamilton has arrived. She's expected," Lord Percy said to the tall, thin servant.

"Very good, my lord," he intoned and withdrew.

Kate felt dull and drab in the gray spencer that she wore over a matching woolen gown compared to Lord Percy, whose attire was in the extravagant mode of the London dandy set. While he was no older than Kate, in his colorful clothes and with his jaunty manner, he seemed like a perennial youth who would never grow old.

Kate pushed aside the absurd thought and edged to the front of the sofa and craned her neck for a peek at the lake through the tall windows. "The view from here is spectacular," she said.

He laughed in a sudden change of mood.

"Spectacular," he echoed suggestively, looking pointedly at her, not the lake.

Kate became flushed. Although she had little practice interacting with men, she recognized flirting when she saw it. His mischievous blue eyes were framed by the longest, thickest lashes she had ever seen on a male.

In another mercurial shift, he gazed toward the door and leaned closer toward her.

"Lord Marchand is vexed with me," he said in a confiding tone. "You must excuse him if he seems out of sorts this morning. Some misunderstanding concerning his sailboat."

Kate heard crisp footsteps in the hall. Lord Percy turned in their direction and she followed his eyes to the doorway, realizing that her absorption with the dandy had caused her to forget why she was here.

But Lord Marchand came into the room as a solid reminder. He was dark-haired, a bit taller than his brother-in-law, and nearer to Mr. Nealy's age than Lord Percy's.

"I am Marchand, Miss Hamilton," he said in a businesslike tone. His apparel was costly, but conservative.

"I am pleased to know you, my lord," Kate said.

When she made to rise, he said, "Sit, sit," more distracted, it appeared, than rude. Kate sensed his curtness was not directed at her.

Her supposition bore fruit when he turned to his brother-in-law and growled, "I thought you left."

Lord Percy did not look the least bit affronted by the viscount's brusqueness. But Lord Marchand's posture made Kate uneasy.

"I did . . . once," Lord Percy said. "However, when I opened the front door, Miss Hamilton and I nearly collided on the porch. I showed the young lady inside and rang for Spakes to fetch you. It would have been unmannerly to have left her unattended."

"Well, she is attended to now, so leave."

Kate was shocked by Lord Marchand's surly manner. Lord Percy's explanation had been reasonable and hardly warranted such a rude response.

The young dandy, to his credit, preserved his composure, got up, and bowed to Kate. "Miss Hamilton," he murmured. He took several steps toward the door and turned. "Addison, I swear your pique is rooted in a misunderstanding. I would have returned the *Pegasus* last night rather than this morning had I known those were your orders."

Lord Marchand excused himself to Kate and moved to Lord Percy's side. Smoothly and efficiently, he grasped the young man's arm, and propelled him toward the vestibule, saying, "Allow me to escort you to the door, Percy."

Kate wished herself somewhere else when Lord Marchand's angry voice carried from the hall.

"Your wits have gone begging if you think I believe you, Percy. I know you were anchored in the lake all night with that hussy from the tavern." Kate put her hands over her ears. She did not want to hear this.

"Did you have your telescope fixed on me?" Lord Percy's melodious voice was tinged with sarcasm. "I never suspected you of being a voyeur, brother-in-law."

"Get out," Lord Marchand ordered. Lord Percy made some indistinct retort. The front door opened and banged closed.

The viscount marched back into the drawing room, mumbling under his breath. "If he harmed that boat I will ring his pretty neck." Kate wanted to leave. She was embarrassed to be witness to a sordid family squabble.

Lord Marchand cleared his throat and sat down in the chair which Lord Percy had vacated. He began to look uncomfortable.

"Forgive me, Miss Hamilton. I had the *Pegasus* especially built for use on the lake. My brother-in-law took her without permission. But I should have curbed my temper in your presence." Not even his apology was enough to overcome the awkwardness or the knot in Kate's stomach.

Lord Marchand cleared his throat for the second time and frowned. "Lord Percy did not annoy you, did he?"

"No, of course not," Kate replied and wished that the viscount would get on with the interview. He was not making a very good impression on her, and she was beginning to be sorry that she had ever come.

Fortunately, at that moment, his wife swept into the room, and sent Kate a polite smile that made her feel better. The viscountess was a petite, blond, pleasant-faced woman. She shook out the folds of her plain cherry crepe dress and sat down next to Kate. Her only jewelry was her wedding ring, its emeralds set in gold.

Lord Marchand had risen in deference to his wife and remained standing, his hands clasped behind his back, allowing her to conduct the interview.

Kate recited the particulars of her education under her scholarly father's tutelage. Lady Marchand seemed satisfied after some probing that Kate was qualified to teach. Her lack of experience came into question, but Kate agreed when the viscountess offered the position on a trial basis and at a salary below that of a qualified governess.

The duties were hardly onerous, teaching in the morning

and supervising playtime in the afternoon. Kate even found the money reasonable, since she was to continue to live with her grandparents.

Lord Marchand had moved to the window shortly after his wife began to question Kate and had stood looking down to where his boat was moored at the dock. He now turned and spoke to Kate for the first time since Lady Marchand began the interview.

"Frankly Miss Hamilton," he said, "your age and your connection to the Franklins works in your favor. Joseph is a fine man and a valued employee. If your work ethic is as strong as his and Mrs. Franklin's, you cannot help but suit."

His good humor seemed restored. He even smiled at Kate.

"Should your services prove to be satisfactory this summer, we can talk later about taking you to London with us in the fall as my girls' permanent governess at a substantially higher wage."

The carrot boosted Kate's spirits as nothing else could have. "Thank you, my lord," she said. "I appreciate the opportunity to prove my worth."

"Well said." The viscount hesitated. "Please put the contretemps with my brother-in-law from your mind, Miss Hamilton. I am not as ill-bred as I must have appeared." Surprisingly, his eyes were lightly mischievous as he met hers. "I promise that I shall never snarl at you."

Kate knew that most aristocrats were not in the habit of considering the sensibilities of their employees. She was forging an agreeable response when Lady Marchand interrupted.

"Oh, Addison, you had words with Percy again. Please tell me you were not too hard on him," she pleaded in a plaintive tone.

"Ida, your brother is a man, not a child to be placated, but this is not the time to discuss his follies," he replied, but with none of the heat or bad temper which had been in evidence earlier. "I will leave you to set a time for Miss Hamilton to begin her duties and meet the girls."

Lady Marchand's concerned eyes followed her husband's retreating back. She gave Kate a tepid false smile. "Elinor and Jane begged to accompany our maid Lucy to the village to pick up some sundries and are not back yet. I will make them known to you tomorrow. Please, be here at eight o'clock, Miss Hamilton," she said, stood up, and offered her hand to indicate the interview was over.

From the crest of the hill, Kate took another look at the lake, which sparkled in the bright sunshine. Lord Marchand was checking the lines on his sailboat. She could read the name *Pegasus* on the stern and watched him yank on the furled sails and poke at the canvas. Near the dock was a strip of sandy beach.

Kate felt a small shock when she saw Lord Percy come through the French doors onto the terrace of the lake house that was closest to the beach. Three years ago, she knew, that particular house had been occupied by an elderly couple, but he must own it now.

Lord Percy was a feast for the eyes. Every young girl in London must surely be in love with him. He leaned on the rail and looked over the water to where Lord Marchand inspected his sailboat.

Kate knew nothing about Lord Percy, but she had seen Lord Marchand as a youth when he had summered here with his father, the Earl of Keith, and his lady mother, but she had never spoken to him before. Her father's illness had restricted her visits to only a few over the past eight years, and she could not remember ever seeing the viscount even in church or in the village during those infrequent trips.

Kate turned from the lake and walked toward home, determined to take Lord Marchand's advice and put the harsh words that had passed between the viscount and Lord Percy from her mind. It was really none of her business.

Her thoughts shifted to another man. Daniel Nealy deserved her thanks. Were it not for him, she would not be on the road to becoming an independent woman. She had a salaried position and a promise of a promotion if she did well.

Kate was happier than she had been at any time since that sorrowful day when her father's heart had finally given out after his long illness. She wanted to share her joy with someone. Her grandparents had opposed her being a governess at all and had been only lukewarm about her taking the position with the Marchands. She would seek out Daniel Nealy. Somehow she knew that he would be truly happy for her.

Three

Lady Marchand presented Elinor and Jane to Kate the next morning. The blond, blue-eyed twins eyed their new governess with frank stares. Their pixie faces were similar, but not identical, making it easy to tell them apart.

Kate had the look of a proper governess in a pewter gown, her rich brown hair pulled into a tidy bun.

"With your lady mother's consent," she said, her hands on her knees and bent to their level, "I would be pleased if you would show me to the schoolroom."

The viscountess agreed and issued a gentle warning to her daughters to behave themselves and to work diligently on their lessons.

"Yes, Mama," the children said in unison, but Kate noticed that Elinor rolled her eyes. Yet it was she who stepped forward and said, "I will show Miss Hamilton the way."

Kate took her leave of Lady Marchand and walked to where Elinor, who had been joined by Jane, waited for her by the door.

With the twins leading the way, Kate climbed the two flights of stairs to the well-appointed schoolroom, which was tucked into a corner of the third floor.

Narrow cupboards held copybooks and ink pots, pens, and slates and chalk. A world map was tacked on a wall beside a casement window, which had been thrown open to let in the morning breeze. Numerous books filled a long shelf on the wall opposite the fireplace.

Elinor and Jane took turns pointing out these features to Kate. She examined the books and was delighted to find many were of a recent acquisition.

"The large desk over by the window is yours, Miss Hamilton," Elinor said, helpfully. "The table is for messy activities like painting and gluing things and this desk is mine and that one is Janie's." She put a possessive hand on her child-sized piece of furniture and pointed with a small finger to her sister's desk, a duplicate of hers.

The children maintained their affability even when Kate immediately put them to work practicing their penmanship by writing the alphabet in their copybooks.

She watched over their shoulders for a time to be certain the assignment was not beyond their capabilities before she moved to the teacher's desk to see if Miss Bennett had left written plans which Kate could use as a guide for her future lessons.

Neatly arranged on the surface of the desk were an iron inkstand, a container of sand for blotting, a metal dish set over a candleholder for melting sealing wax, a box of chalk, a quill pen, and some blank paper.

Kate pulled out the desk chair, sat down, and opened each of the three side drawers, but found all of them empty.

Elinor cleaned the nib of her pen on a wiper cloth. "What are you looking for?" she asked Kate.

"I thought Miss Bennett may have kept records of your progress," she said. "I would like to have some idea of how far you have advanced in the subjects you have studied."

Elinor went to the bookcase and pulled out a ledger. "Is this what you want?" she asked, offering the book to Kate.

Kate rifled through the pages. "Yes, thank you, Elinor. This is exactly what I was seeking." Miss Bennett had noted the numbers of the pages the children had covered in their various textbooks and other pertinent comments about their scholastic attainments.

Elinor returned to her desk, but did not pick up her pen. "Miss Bennett wasn't our governess for long," she said. "Before she came, we had a nanny until we turned eight a few months ago. Miss Bennett left suddenly when she claimed that she was needed at home to nurse her sick mother."

Claimed? Kate picked up on the revealing word. But she checked her curiosity as inappropriate. The circumstances of Miss Bennett's termination of employment were none of her affair. She shoved herself up from the desk chair and walked over to the twins' desks to monitor the children's writing assignment.

Before she could bend down to examine their work, Jane said, "Miss Bennett would get all flustered when Uncle Percy came to observe us in the schoolroom. We heard Cook say that was why she left us. I guess it could be true."

Elinor made a sound that could only be described as a snort. "It *is* true," she said, importantly. "No one was sick, not her mother, nobody. Uncle Percy *drove* Miss Bennett away. Cook said so."

Taken aback by the unseemly direction of the twins' conversation, Kate chided, "I do not think your parents would approve of your gossiping with the kitchen staff."

"We didn't," Jane said. "We heard Cook when we passed by the kitchen door."

"You should not be eavesdropping," Kate pointed out.

Elinor lifted an indignant eyebrow. "It is not our fault if the servants' loud voices carry right through the door."

Kate nearly laughed at the ingenuous remark, but managed to look suitably sober. "But you are in the wrong if you pass on the tittle-tattle, as you did to me. In my experience, gossip is often based on misconceptions or half-truths. I, for one, do not want to hear malicious stories from you. Ever. Do you understand?"

"Yes," Jane said, immediately. Elinor's acquiescent nod was coated with a thin veneer of rebellion and she took a moment longer, but she finally said, "All right," but none too graciously.

Kate's face lightened a little. "Thank you, ladies," she said in a tone meant to soothe. "Now, let us see if you can write a full line of cursive letters without blotting your copybooks."

Elinor dipped her pen point into the pot of black ink. She wrote a capital D, on the line where she had left off on her assignment earlier.

"Miss Hamilton, you are prettier than Miss Bennett," she said, shamelessly fawning.

Kate could not contain a chuckle. "I am immune to false compliments, Lady Elinor," she said. "Well, almost."

Both Elinor and Jane giggled. The bad moment was over.

"Oh, Mr. Nealy, how providential to find you on my doorstep!"

Kate had just stepped from the carriage house into the gathering dusk of early evening to walk Penny, her grandmother's spaniel.

Mr. Nealy smiled, clearly pleased to see her. "What an intriguing greeting, Miss Hamilton. Let us walk together and you can explain yourself while we exercise the dogs. This fellow is getting on in years, but he still likes his run."

The *fellow* that he referred to was a coal black, medium-sized dog of uncertain ancestry that he called Prince.

Kate and Daniel strolled off together down the lane, the dogs running ahead and nosing into the undergrowth that was dotted with bluebells and purple violets.

"I sought you out yesterday," Kate said, "but my grandfather told me you were at Farmer Thull's assisting a mare in a difficult birth. I wanted you to know that Lord Marchand hired me as the governess to Elinor and Jane."

"How perfectly splendid!" Mr. Nealy exclaimed, exactly as Kate had imagined that he would.

She looked up at his strong face. "I owe it all to you, sir, for interceding with the viscount."

Mr. Nealy's brown eyes gleamed appreciatively as he glanced down into her upturned face, but he said, "It was a small matter."

Kate did not think so, although she accepted his demur, sensing that he was the sort of man who would be ill at ease with lavish praise.

"Lady Marchand was courteous and kind and the viscount promised to consider me for the position of the children's full-time governess at summer's end."

"I knew that you would acquit yourself admirably," he said, giving her a verbal pat on the back.

Kate chose not to say any more about the interview, which was fraught with pitfalls. There was the squabble between Lord Percy Westcott and Lord Marchand, Lady Marchand's concern for her brother, and even Lord Percy's curiosity about Kate's relationship with Mr. Nealy. She really did not want to talk about any of those things.

Instead she said, "Before I assumed my schoolroom duties, I had two fears. First, that the children would resent my taking Miss Bennett's place and, second, that the girls would test my resolve by pulling pranks on me. Neither dread came to pass."

He chuckled. "I would not become too complacent about the pulling of pranks, for such behavior can increase with familiarity."

Sounding more thoughtful, he added, "I do not believe Elinor and Jane ever became overly fond of Miss Bennett."

"I want to do a good job," Kate said.

"You shall. You know, Miss Bennett was inexperienced and much too young for the position. But she was a distant connection of Lord Marchand's mother's. You are more mature, Miss Hamilton, and have more common sense."

More common sense? His cryptic remark begged for clarification, but the dogs yelped excitedly and ran around in circles in the low brush.

"Oh, oh, trouble," Mr. Nealy said. "The dogs have unearthed a small animal and are chasing it."

He put two fingers to his lips and let out a shrill whistle. Prince dashed back to him. Penny, however, ignored Kate's frantic entreaties.

"I'll get her," Mr. Nealy said and plunged into the bracken after the spaniel and came back holding her by the collar.

"No harm," he said, brushing at his black breeches. "The rabbit bolted into its hole."

Kate looked up at the rising half-moon. "We better go back," she said. "It is getting dark."

Quite struck by Prince's instant obedience to Mr. Nealy's commands, Kate complimented him on his dog's exemplary behavior.

"I don't own Prince," he said. "His elderly mistress developed severe rheumatism. She sold her lake house and now lives in a home for the aged and infirmed and asked me to look after the dog for her."

"He certainly is well-behaved," Kate said, much impressed.

Mr. Nealy smiled. "He is now. Prince was a spoiled brat of a dog when he came to me. It took me a full month of intensive training to teach him manners and to respond promptly to my commands."

Kate smiled, too. "Apparently, you disproved that old adage that you can't teach an old dog new tricks, but in one month?"

"For some reason animals and I have always understood each other," he said, as if it were the most natural thing in the world. "I trained my own dogs from an age when I was barely out of leading strings."

"Such a talent must give you a leg up in your profession,"

Kate remarked. "You do not lack for steady employment, true?" She gasped. "Oh, dear, that sounds impertinent."

"Now who's prying?" he said with a chuckle. "But, yes, Miss Hamilton, I do keep busy. Trained animal doctors are scarce. There are numerous farms and estates within a reasonable radius to keep me working constantly. Then, there is the continual custom from the residents in the houses along the lake who call on me to treat their pet dogs and their horses."

The moon had climbed high into the sky by the time they reached the door to the carriage house.

"You seem quite settled into the district," Kate said. "Do you think you will make your permanent home here?"

"Yes, I do. I love this part of the country and like the people very much. I plan to buy a lake house as soon as one goes on the market."

Kate put her hand on the doorknob. Mr. Nealy would have to doctor thousands of sick creatures to save enough money to buy a lake house, but she was too well-mannered to say such a thing. But that was silly. He came from a wealthy family and, certainly, did not depend on his vocation to earn his bread.

He whistled Prince to his side and bid Kate good night, his parting congenial.

Kate let Penny into the carriage house. The spaniel scrambled up the stairs, drawn by her elderly owners' familiar voices, which drifted down from the parlor.

Kate stood at the door and watched Mr. Nealy cross the yard to the stone cottage which had been the gamekeeper's house when the estate was prosperous. According to her grandmother, Mr. Nealy had restored the long-abandoned property, inside and outside, all by himself, scrubbing and painting for long hours, even after putting in a full day's work, Cloris had said.

He closed the door, and Kate did the same and went upstairs.

Even on such short acquaintance, she had formed

some opinions about him. He was dependable and democratically impartial where people were concerned. She smiled a little. Moreover, he was not afraid of hard work, which was certainly an uncommon commodity among the peerage.

Four

Lord Percy Westcott leaned against the frame of the schoolroom door, languidly swinging to and fro the quizzing glass which hung on a gold ribbon about his handsome neck.

Elinor and Jane sat at the table with their backs to their uncle, concentrating on sketching a wild daisy as part of their nature studies.

Kate's gaze lingered on Lord Percy for too long to be casual interest. His slow, intimate smile caused her heart to flutter. She gave herself a mental shake and pretended to examine her charges' childish drawings before she lifted her eyes a notch to take a furtive glance in his direction, only to find him gone.

She felt deserted. What idiocy, she thought and shook her head to revive her sanity.

But the following day, Lord Percy, splendid in a periwinkle superfine coat, was back and bolder. He invited himself into the schoolroom, took a seat at the teacher's desk, and commanded Kate to carry on with her lesson.

Kate was aware that his eyes dwelled on her more than on Elinor and Jane. She talked herself into believing that he was concerned with his nieces' schooling and was observing her teaching methods, perhaps even at Lady Marchand's behest.

Kate's delusion lasted a single day, for on the third day Lord Percy brought chaos to the schoolroom. He played the clown with the children and bantered with Kate. His enthusiasm for mischief proved contagious. Elinor and Jane fell into fits of irrepressible giggles at his silly jokes. Kate was not immune to his outrageous humor and laughed until her sides split. Her halfhearted battle to teach a geography lesson turned into a fiasco.

Thoroughly ashamed at having lost control the previous day, Kate knew she must ban Lord Percy from the schoolroom. When she arrived fifteen minutes before Elinor and Jane were due for their lessons, he was already seated at her desk.

"Your frivolous antics are too disruptive for a schoolroom, my lord," she said in a mild reproof. "I, too, am at fault for behaving like a ninny who does not have the least notion of how to go on in her job. I am afraid that Elinor and Jane will learn nothing if I let you stay, so, I must respectfully ask you to leave."

He came to his feet. "You are throwing me out?"

"Not to put too fine a point on it, yes."

"You can't mean it, Miss Hamilton?" His boyish pout was appealing, but Kate remained firm.

"Oh, but I do, my lord," she said, a finger to her chin. She tried to look as confident as though she were accustomed to ordering about peers of the realm on a daily basis.

Lord Percy sighed, but he did not argue.

Kate stared at the door long after he left. She had never known anyone even remotely like him. While she was not an unhappy person, she was mostly serious and had been so even as a child. Then her father's long illness had required her to lead an even more quiet life. She had never gone to balls or parties. Lord Percy was fun and brought out the silly side of her nature. She could not remember ever having laughed so much.

She picked up Elinor's slate and wiped it clean, replaced it on the child's desk, and did the same with Jane's.

If what Cook said was true, Miss Bennett must have misjudged Lord Percy. Kate could see how a young, naive female might have been scandalized by his foolishness.

His reckless spirit could have scared her. But *drove her off* was extremely harsh.

Kate lifted the lids on the ink pots on the children's desks and checked the level of ink and filled Jane's from the jug kept in the storage closet.

Kate was not heartless, but she was convinced that no real harm had been done to Miss Bennett. The former governess had a home to which she could return. Many young women whose posts became insupportable had no recourse but to remain imprisoned in a hateful job. Yet Kate was sure that Miss Bennett had overreacted to Lord Percy's harmless overtures.

She heard the children on the stairs and put Miss Bennett from her mind, smoothed her gray heather skirt, and picked up a history book, determined to make up for her previous day's dereliction of duty.

Lord Percy physically vanished from Kate's world, but not from her thoughts. She became worried that she was in his black books for ejecting him from the schoolroom. Guilt-ridden, she wondered if she had been too overbearing. Could she have been more tactful? Perhaps she should have permitted him to remain if he had promised to behave himself. Smiling at some remembered nonsense of his, she yearned to restore the incipient friendship that had been developing between them.

So when Lord Percy intercepted her as she left the main house for home two days later, Kate was overjoyed to see him. His charming smile was irresistible, although his flame red coat, purple vest, and canary breeches abused the eye.

"I'll walk with you if I may," he said.

Kate gave her permission, whereupon he fell into step beside her.

"Tell me something of your background, Miss Hamilton," he said, in a perfectly modulated voice after a bit of casual conversation. Today his tone was not mischievous or teasing, but politely respectful. "Your father carried a title, I have heard."

"Yes, the king honored him for his archeological discoveries," Kate said proudly. "He became Sir Matthew and, my mother, Lady Charlotte. But, by then, their habits were set and rubbing elbows with people of first respectability held no appeal for either of them."

Lord Percy regarded her with an incredulous expression. "How strange," he said. "Your parents did not care to better themselves?"

Kate was certain that her scholarly father and her country bred mother would not have been happy rubbing elbows with the *ton,* nor would they have considered it *bettering themselves.*

"My parents cared more for academic pursuits than for polite society," she said, thinking, but not saying, that making a mark among the powerful also took money, of which there had never been much in her father's family.

"What of your own aspirations, Miss Hamilton?" he asked.

Kate thought it a rather strange question to ask a female, but she answered, "To be a qualified governess, to your nieces for now. Later . . . well." She shrugged.

"Yes, later," he said. "I trust you do not lack ambition. Or are you like Daniel Nealy with his wrongheaded notions that working like a peasant is somehow noble?"

Kate let this pass, for lack of a response, but he spoke again.

"You are quite pretty, Miss Hamilton." Kate blushed, but the compliment was clouded when he added, "You also have a lovely figure. You know, many a sharp-witted female of small means has used these assets to her benefit."

Kate was not an idiot. Lord Percy was hinting that she could use her wiles to snare some wealthy older gentleman into a marriage that would be above her station. She couldn't take umbrage, for the practice was accepted by the *ton.*

However, her lack of contact with gentlemen of his ilk, put her at a disadvantage as to where to draw the line on personal comments. She suspected that his mention of her *lovely figure* was inappropriate. It was time to change the subject.

"Lord Marchand will take me to London in the fall as the twins' governess if I prove myself worthy of the promotion," she said, keeping her composure cool.

"What a laudable goal." His tone bordered on mockery. "Yet, perhaps once you are in the City you will tire of being a governess and look for a more lucrative position."

Whereupon, he waved an abrupt farewell, leaving Kate thoroughly confused. She took the path through the trees that led to the carriage house, her forehead furrowed in a puzzled frown. Lord Percy seemed to be intimating something that was completely lost on her.

Five

The downstairs door opened and Kate heard Mr. Nealy call up the stairs, "It's me, Daniel." He bounded up the steps without a formal invitation.

Kate stood in the doorway between the kitchen and the parlor.

He smiled and said, "Miss Hamilton," but strode past her across the parlor floor to where Joseph sat beside the fire.

Mr. Nealy's legs were long and strong, his stride confident. There was something solid about the veterinarian that Kate found appealing.

He shook hands with Joseph before he walked back to Kate.

"You have been gone for a few days," she said.

"You missed me, Miss Hamilton?" He looked far too pleased.

Kate rolled her eyes heavenward. "Do not let it go to your head, Mr. Nealy. I just wondered why Grandpa was taking care of Prince."

He laughed heartily and feigned a sigh. "Putting me in my place, eh?" He bent down to look at the fading rash on Penny's legs when the dog wiggled up to him.

Cloris Franklin came from the kitchen, wiping her hands on her brown cotton apron.

"Penny's infection seems to be clearing up nicely, Mrs. Cloris," Mr. Nealy said and stood up straight and tall.

"Aye, Daniel, the salve works. You can safely purchase from that vendor who gave you the samples," she said.

"That I can," he agreed, his smile genuine. "Thank you for inviting me to supper. Your meals are always exceptional."

Cloris chuckled. "Exceptional? Now there's a word I don't often hear around here."

Kate smiled. Mr. Nealy was no stranger to Cloris's cooking, she knew. He had supped with the Franklins any number of times since he had come to work in the district.

Kate moved into the kitchen. She took a basket of brown bread from the sideboard and placed it on the stout table set for four.

Mr. Nealy braced a broad shoulder against the doorjamb between the two rooms and watched her.

Kate felt it was incumbent on her to start a conversation with him since he was a guest. "You attended a conference in London at the Royal Veterinary College, I hear," she said, straightening the silverware, which did not need straightening.

He responded with a light answer that led her to believe that he felt she would be bored were he to go into details about a subject she might find dry.

Kate could see why Joseph and Cloris respected him. He was not full of himself, but considerate of others. But her curiosity had been aroused, and she asked him some pertinent questions about veterinary medicine and found that his answers were neither dull nor tiresome, but interesting.

Cloris turned from the stove where she had been stirring bacon into the green beans while listening to them.

"'T'would not be amiss, I think, if you became Daniel and Kate to each other," she said. "Sounds rather queer to me to have you being so formal with one another in this house."

Kate found this agreeable, but waited for Mr. Nealy to speak first.

"If Miss Hamilton is willing," he said, gallantly, "it would be my honor."

Kate gave her permission, allowing a smile to sound in her voice. She heard Cloris sigh. Her grandmother would be pleased, she knew, if Kate and the veterinarian formed an attachment. Mr. Nealy, Daniel, was a comfortable man who would make a fine friend, but Kate was not at all sure she could ever fall in love with him.

Cloris called Joseph to supper, and everyone sat down to the superb meal of roast beef, crusty new potatoes, and vegetables. Talk flowed effortlessly, for Daniel's occupation sparked his own keen interest in rural matters, which formed the old couple's whole world.

Daniel and Joseph retired to the parlor and continued their conversation over a glass of port while Kate and her grandmother cleaned up the kitchen.

When the dishes had been put away, Kate took off her apron and went into the parlor to fetch her wraps and Penny for the spaniel's nightly walk.

Daniel rose from his chair by the fire. "I will leave now, too," he said. "I have an early call to make on Squire Colchester's bull."

He tendered his compliments to the cook and thanked his host for his hospitality before following Kate and the dog down the stairs. But once outside, he said to Kate, "Wait here. I will go across to my house and get Prince and join you."

A light mist drifted up from the lake. Kate gathered her warm woolen cape around her against the cold and watched Daniel as he came toward her with the black mongrel at his heels. He smiled down at Penny, who ran circles around him and Prince.

Kate liked Daniel's lean, tan face. Of course, he could not compare to Lord Percy in looks, but, then, who could? But he was easy to talk to and good company.

* * *

During the walk, Daniel said, "I heard a rumor this afternoon at the village tavern that Lord Wiggens was putting his lake house on the market. I called on the baron immediately, but he has not made a definite decision yet and won't entertain offers, but he did promise me first refusal when he does."

"So you are really serious about purchasing a lake property," Kate remarked.

"Oh, yes, decidedly," he answered.

"I always thought bachelors preferred smaller accommodations, but it seems not. Lord Percy Westcott lives all alone in that charming lake house."

Daniel stopped in his tracks, where thin fog crawled over the ground at his feet.

"You have been in Percy's house?" he asked, looking down at her, a deep frown between his brows.

"No, of course, I have not," she said, rather taken aback. "He is a bachelor. I meant charming from the outside."

"But you have met him," he said. "Of course, you have." His voice became faintly urgent. "Has he been annoying you?" Oddly, she had heard the same question from Lord Marchand.

"No." Kate put as much conviction as she could into the single word denial. He did not need to know about Lord Percy's disruptions of her schoolroom lessons, in which she had been a willing accomplice. And, in all fairness, when she had asked the young dandy to stay away, he had complied. She had no reason to complain about Lord Percy. Even if she did have, it was none of Daniel's business.

Kate said as much to him. "Lord Percy has done nothing to which I would take offense. But, frankly, sir, my encounters with him are not your concern. I can take care of myself. I am hardly a milk and water miss who would be susceptible to a gentleman simply because he has a very handsome face."

Daniel studied her for a moment after she had stopped

speaking before he burst out laughing. "You find Percy *very* handsome, do you?"

Kate's self-possession cracked. She grinned. "Daniel," she said, slowly, "a woman would have to be blind not to notice his perfect looks. But it doesn't mean I am going to go all soft in the head over him."

"My misapprehension," he said, the laughter still in his brown eyes.

Although their conversation was sparse, their walk was surprisingly relaxing. Kate started to bid Daniel good night at her grandparents' door, but he stopped her, his hand covering hers on the doorknob.

"Come with me on Saturday to pay a call on Prince's mistress," he said. "Hannah Morgan stays at a home for the aged and infirm. The dear old lady has no family and lives for the days when I can bring Prince to visit her. I would welcome your company on the ride."

"Oh, Daniel," Kate said, wishing she could go, "I normally have Saturdays free, but the adults at the main house are going across the lake to the Smythes' cottage for a day of sailing and picnicking. Lady Marchand has asked me to keep the children."

"Bring Jane and Elinor along," Daniel said without a moment's hesitation. "I daresay Mrs. Morgan would love to see the girls. She knew them when they were mere babes. On the way back, we can have our own picnic beside the lake. I will even arrange for the food."

Kate gave him a questioning look. "Is a home for the aged and infirmed a place to take children?"

"It is not as you think, Kate. I meet Mrs. Morgan in a pleasant garden because of the dog. Elinor and Jane would not be exposed to the wards where the truly sick and lame are housed."

Kate wanted to go. She liked Daniel very much and

welcomed an opportunity to spend a day with him. She paused and considered.

Taking advantage of her hesitation, Daniel said, "I will clear it with Addison. What do you say?"

"Well," she said slowly, "if Lord Marchand permits it, of course, I say yes."

"Good," Daniel said. "I will make the arrangements."

He leaned down and dropped a kiss on her cheek, whistled Prince to his side, and vanished into the thickening fog.

Kate lifted a hand to the cheek his warm lips had touched. His butterfly kiss had felt so very sweet. What a lovely man Daniel Nealy was, she thought, and hoped that Lord Marchand would agree to the Saturday outing.

On Friday afternoon Kate took Elinor and Jane to the sandy beach at the lake to play. Daniel had apparently wasted no time in petitioning the viscount, for the twins were chattering happily about going to see Mrs. Morgan and picnicking by the lake.

"Mr. Nealy has invited us just as if we were grown-ups," Elinor said, a little in awe, bringing a smile to Kate's face.

She wondered if Daniel Nealy ever put his foot wrong. Not that he was a sobersides. Far from it. His humor was not overt like Lord Percy's. Mostly it lurked in his brown eyes and came out subtly in his speech.

Kate left the twins to their tin pails and shovels and spread a blanket on the sand nearby for herself. She sat down, resting her back against a smooth rock, and opened the novel she had bought at Hatchard's before she left London.

Dressed appropriately for play on the beach, the children were determined to build a sandcastle like the one in a picture book. Their pinafores were old, as were their shoes. The sunbonnets, which covered their blond heads, were tied securely beneath their chins.

Jane carried water in her pail from the lake to the chosen site, while Elinor sculpted the wet sand into mounds.

Kate was lost in Mr. Scott's latest adventure and had
been only marginally aware of the children's voices for
some time when Elinor shouted, "Uncle Percy!"

Kate's heart lost a beat. Elinor and Jane abandoned
their project and ran toward Lord Percy, who had come
down to the beach from his lake house and was walking
in their direction.

Elinor was the first to reach her uncle. He jumped back
to avoid her outstretched hand before she could touch the
sleeve of his emerald coat, which he wore over immacu-
late yellow-and-white striped trousers.

"Good grief, wash your filthy little hands before you at-
tack me, " he said, rather more amicably than his words
would have indicated.

Kate put her book down and peered from beneath her
wide-brimmed sun hat at Lord Percy. His superior golden
looks never ceased to amaze her. He tipped his fashionable
straw boater and said, "Miss Hamilton. Mind if I join
you?"

The request was apparently rhetorical, for he made himself comfortable immediately on the edge of the blanket,
his knees drawn up.

"My lord," Kate managed in way of a greeting, as she
rummaged in a canvas bag for towels and gave them to the
children, who had swished the sand from their hands in the
clear lake water and now stood before their uncle.

Elinor held out her clean palms for Lord Percy to examine. "Swing me over the water," she begged, jiggling up
and down.

Kate assumed that Elinor referred to a game, unknown
to Kate, but familiar to both Elinor and her uncle.

"Later, poppet," Lord Percy said, confirming Kate's as-
sumption. "Right now I want to speak with Miss Hamilton."

"Do you promise?" Elinor's small chin was set mulishly.

"Insolent minx." He winked at her. "M'word of honor

as a gentleman. " He took in both her and Jane with the promise.

"See that tall pine just this side of Lord Clark's property? Walk there. When you come back, I'll swing each of you over the lake."

The twins ran off, Elinor in the lead. Lord Percy shouted, "Slowly, walk slowly. Or it don't count." The girls adjusted their stride to a more leisurely pace.

Kate smiled as she shook out the children's towels and tucked them back into her bag, along with her book.

Lord Percy reminded her of a boy who never wanted to grow up when he said, "That got 'em," with a silly grin.

But his next words brought them back into the world of adults. "My brother-in-law's behavior on the day I met you was the outside of enough." His handsome lips thinned into a tight line. "Addison becomes completely irrational when it comes to the *Pegasus*. My sister gave me permission to use the sailboat but forgot to tell him. Can you imagine; he accused her of covering up for me."

Kate did not want to be dragged into their family squabble a second time. "Please, my lord," she said. "You need not explain."

"But I do," he insisted. "Our voices must have carried to you from the vestibule. Addison besmirched my good name by linking me to a woman of suspect morals. I want you to know the hussy was a figment of his imagination. I was night-fishing all on my own."

Lord Percy's sincere indignation convinced Kate that he was telling the truth. She brushed some sand from her practical dark skirt and said, "I regret that Lord Marchand berated you unfairly."

"Thank you," Lord Percy said, sighed soulfully, and lowered his wonderful blue eyes. His long lashes curled onto his perfect cheek and Kate thought he looked adorable.

"I believe that your lake house was one of the last ones built," she said to divert his thoughts as well as her own.

"When I was here to visit my grandparents three years ago, your cottage was inhabited by an older couple, I believe."

"Yes," Lord Percy said. "I befriended the widow after her husband died, for no one else seemed to care about her when her health deteriorated. Eventually, she decided to sell. I liked the house, but I ended up paying a premium to keep her from being cheated by an unscrupulous agent."

"What a selfless gesture," Kate said, praising his generosity, but he was looking off over her shoulder.

"Our peace is about to be disturbed," he said. "The twins have completed their fool's errand."

Elinor's patience had clearly run out when she stopped in front of her uncle. "We are back. Now you must keep your word, Uncle Percy."

He got up with a moan and followed Elinor to the water's edge, where she turned her back to her uncle and raised her arms to the side. He snatched her under the armpits and swung her back and forth over the lake while she screamed in delight.

Jane was next. When both twins had had a turn, Elinor jumped up and down in front of Lord Percy, who was gazing rather forlornly down at his shoes.

"Do it again, Uncle Percy," she cried.

"Can't," he said. "As it is, I stepped in the water. I shall have to endure a fierce scold from my valet for ruining the shine on my shoes."

Elinor giggled. "I know, give Miss Hamilton a turn."

Lord Percy forgot his footwear and got a wicked gleam in his eyes. "Hmm," he mused as Kate stiffened under his impish gaze.

"My lord, you would not dare." Kate's voice squeaked unnaturally.

"No?" He wiggled his fingers in a come-hither gesture.

He pulled her up from the blanket by her wrists while she protested loudly.

"Please, sir. Stop. This is unseemly. My reputation."

He released her. Kate breathed a sigh of relief, but not for long.

Lord Percy beckoned the twins to his side. "Raise your right hands, ladies. Do you solemnly swear to protect Miss Hamilton's reputation by keeping this our secret for ever and ever?"

"Yes!" the twins shouted in unison, warming to the grand game.

The next moment, Kate found herself in Lord Percy's arms. He had lifted her from the ground as her father had done when he had carried her to bed as a small child.

Kate stopped struggling, finding it undignified to fight with him, but she kept up her pleading. He held her close to his chest and whirled her around in dizzying circles, her anger growing with his increasingly outlandish behavior. The verbal protests proved useless. She held on for dear life, one hand clutching his neck and the other smashed on top of her hat to keep it from falling off.

To add to her humiliation, the twins were whooping and cavorting around them like wild creatures.

Kate's heart was pounding with rage when Lord Percy finally stopped. But, of one thing she was aware. His warm lips had slid down her cheek just before he set her down on rubbery legs.

Elinor ran up to them and balled her fists on her hips.

"No fair! No fair!" she shouted. "You did not swing Miss Hamilton over the lake."

Kate had had enough from the two children. No, three, she amended. Lord Percy was nothing but a naughty overgrown boy.

"Playtime is over," she said, her tone peevish. "Pick up your toys. We must go home now and get cleaned up for your music lesson."

The children mumbled under their breaths, but obeyed.

Kate avoided Lord Percy's eyes. She picked up the canvas bag and set it to the side while she briskly shook the sand from the blanket and folded it into a neat square.

Lord Percy had his hands deep in the pockets of his modish trousers. "I expect you are wishing me to Jericho," he said, softly contrite.

"You behaved foolishly, my lord," she said, still angry. "The beach is exposed to public view."

Kate shuddered inwardly. Suppose they had been seen. Her grandparents would be undone if her name was linked scandalously with Lord Percy's.

Kate wanted to lash out at him, but his expression was so pathetic, sad, and remorseful that she went soft.

"I have not taken you in disgust," she said in a tone she would have used with a willful boy who was truly sorry for his misdeeds. "The children do have a music lesson with Mr. Fetters in half an hour."

Kate started after the twins, who were already walking back to the house with their pails and shovels in hand.

"Forgive me, please, Miss Hamilton," he pleaded to her back. "I meant no harm. It was all innocent fun, meant to amuse and entertain Elinor and Jane."

Kate turned around and against all logic she gave him a smile of absolution.

Six

Saturday morning Daniel pulled up in his chaise to the door of the carriage house and looked down from his high perch. Kate had shed her governess's gowns of subdued colors and wore a violet spencer over a lilac skirt.

"What a fetching bonnet," he said with admiration. Kate touched the small brim of her straw hat with its trailing purple ribbons and smiled.

Daniel stretched down his arm and grasped Kate's hand in his own and helped her up onto the seat beside him. Dressed in his usual black attire, which somehow suited him perfectly, he held the horse's reins with his free hand.

"Kate, I must say, the spring hues you chose to wear today suit you very well. You look absolutely lovely," he said. She glowed as she read the truth of his high opinion of her in his brown eyes.

Conscious of the blush that was coming onto her cheeks, Kate turned toward the back seat, where Prince sat erect like royalty. She was absentmindedly giving the black dog a few affectionate pats on his head when she spied a hamper behind the driver's seat.

"I see you brought the lunch," she said, facing front.

"Yes," Daniel said and snapped the reins to set the gray horse in motion. "Do you think we could drive right past the main house and pretend that we forgot Elinor and Jane?"

Kate laughed. "I don't think that we would get away

with it. It was terribly kind of you to invite them, you know."

His smile wavered. "Do not make me out to be such a virtuous fellow, Kate. Remember, if I could have had you alone, I would not have asked the twins."

She felt a satisfying inner warmth brought on by his words, but she wondered if he was being romantic or simply gallant. And more to the point, which would she prefer? She knew she did not have an answer. But it was nice to be admired.

Daniel's chaise rolled to a stop in front of the main house, where the twins anxiously waited in their pink coats and matching bonnets. Elinor and Jane tumbled down the steps and ran to the chaise and climbed into the backseat, talking over each other while exchanging greetings with Kate and Daniel.

After taking a quick look into the backseat to make sure that his passengers were ready to depart, Daniel drove off.

Prince laid his head on Jane's lap, and she obligingly scratched his head for several minutes before she pushed him away. Deprived of Jane's attention, the dog jumped down onto the floorboards, curled into a corner, and went to sleep. He did not awaken until an hour later, when Daniel parked the light vehicle in a designated area for visitors to the Crestview Home for the Aged and Infirmed and secured the horse to a hitching post.

Kate had enjoyed the ride, for Daniel had entertained her and the children with funny stories about some of his more eccentric animal patients. He spun a good tale.

When Daniel helped her and the twins down from the chaise, she was still smiling about the story of the mother cat who had adopted a brood of baby chicks.

"Wait for me here," he said, "while I go inside to arrange for our visit."

The children ran up and down the sidewalk with Prince, but Kate stood beside the chaise and looked around. The old-age home was nothing like any institution she had ever seen before. There were no inhospitable walls here, only tall shade trees, a green lawn, and colorful flower beds that gave a cheerful appearance to the ivy-covered brick building.

Daniel came back and clipped a leash onto Prince's collar. "This way," he said. They passed through a gate on the shady side of the building into a garden that was surrounded by a decorative iron fence which defined rather than imprisoned. In the distance Guernseys grazed in rich, lush pastures.

Mrs. Morgan waved to Daniel from a rolling chair parked under a hickory tree, the lower part of her body covered by a blue afghan.

Daniel led Prince to her chair while Kate and the twins followed close behind. Kate stood back a little, her arms around Elinor's and Jane's shoulders while Hannah Morgan hugged the excited, quivering dog and spoke loving nonsense into his big ears.

Daniel winked at Kate and called her forward when Prince had finally settled himself at Hannah Morgan's feet.

Mrs. Morgan remembered the twins and asked after their parents' health. "My, my, how you two have grown since I last saw you," she said as adults were wont to do of children whom they had not seen for a long time. The twins were polite, but slightly self-conscious, and, in time, Mrs. Morgan turned her attention to Kate.

"You have the look of your grandmother, Miss Hamilton," she said and went on to ask about the Franklins as she had about Lord and Lady Marchand.

Kate and Daniel sat down in the wicker chairs that an attendant had brought outside for them. Kate gave Elinor and Jane permission to walk around, but she kept an eye on them. Soon, however, several of the elderly residents who were taking the air showed an interest in the twins. Before long, Elinor and Jane were talking and laughing with them. With the girls happily occupied, Kate sat back and relaxed as she listened to Daniel and

Mrs. Morgan, who were engaged in some lighthearted chatter.

The spring day was all sunshine and cloudless blue sky. Kate offered a few words, but mostly she enjoyed being outdoors and watching Daniel. She was sure she had never known a man before with such an even and calm disposition.

After a while, Daniel excused himself and went into the brick building through a back door. He had not mentioned the reason, but Mrs. Morgan was quick to fill Kate in.

"Daniel has gone to enact some business for me," she said. "He acts as my guardian since I have no family." She must have noticed Kate's puzzled expression, for she said, "I know what you are thinking, Miss Hamilton. What is a veterinarian doing taking care of my affairs? Our lake house neighbors had always been tolerant, but, otherwise, indifferent to my husband and me because he had made his money in trade. Daniel lacks that sort of snobbery. He came to my aid when my husband died. Once I sold my lake house and came here to live, he simply continued to look after me out the kindness born of a good heart, nothing more. He is that sort of man."

Kate agreed silently with her. Daniel was indeed that sort of man. Mrs. Morgan was fortunate to have him looking after her, a woman unrelated to him, as well as to have the means to be in a rare private nursing home. The moneyed sick who had families were normally nursed at home. Her father, fortunately, had not been bedridden until the last three days of his life, but had been restricted to quiet pursuits. The indigent poor were sent to depressing public hospitals and cared for by overworked and underpaid personnel.

Their eyes met, and Mrs. Morgan gave Kate a small smile, but it was not a happy one.

As though reading Kate's mind, she said, "I know how lucky I am, Miss Hamilton, to have a person as trustworthy as Daniel as a friend. Shortly after I was alone in the world, a charming young gentleman who was more handsome than any man has a right to be began to visit me quite frequently. I was flattered at first. He was highly amusing and put me in a better frame of mind. He advised me to move from the lake for the dampness was not good for my rheumatism. He was right, of course, but he was not interested in my welfare. He began to pressure me to sell him my house, unlike Daniel who never asked anything from me."

Mrs. Morgan did not name the charming gentleman, and Kate did not intend to ask her who he was. A *gentleman more handsome than any man has a right to be* had brought Lord Percy Westcott immediately to Kate's mind. Yet, it could be someone else. But Kate knew that she was fooling herself.

Prince sat up, yawned, and looked around the garden, blinking. Hannah Morgan patted her knee, inviting the dog to put his head on her lap, and she stroked his big black ears.

"I don't know what would have become of you, Prince, if Daniel had not adopted you." Mrs. Morgan had tears in her voice.

Impulsively, Kate touched her arm in a gesture meant to console, but Mrs. Morgan squared her thin shoulders and said, "I am making a cake of myself. I am fortunate to be able to afford to live here where I am well looked after. I should not be complaining."

Kate did not know what to say. The two women sat quietly side by side until Daniel returned, By then, Hannah Morgan was able to offer him a genuine smile.

Later as Daniel bowled down the road in the chaise, Kate said to him, "Mrs. Morgan really loves Prince."

"Yes, she does," he replied. "I wish Hannah had a family where she could live and keep the dog permanently with her, but that is not possible. At least she has the money to afford Crestview, where she is treated with dignity."

Kate was still thinking about Mrs. Morgan when Daniel came upon St. Swithin's, the village church built of weather-beaten fieldstone, and slowed down. Parishioners were leaving the sanctuary and going to their vehicles, which were parked on both sides of the narrow road.

Daniel pulled over and stopped. "I had better wait until the traffic clears, and I have a safe path for my horse."

Elinor leaned forward. "Why are there people at the church?" she wondered. "It isn't Sunday."

"Why, it's a wedding," Kate said, a lift in her voice. "See, the bridal carriage is just leaving." She pointed to a coach that was coming slowly toward them. It was gaily adorned with seasonal flowers and white ribbons. "You will be able to make out the bride and groom inside when it goes by."

The plumed horses moved past them and went off in the direction from which Daniel had come.

"I saw the bride," Elinor cried. "She had a crown of yellow flowers on her head."

"I saw her, too," Jane said, "and the groom had black hair. Remember, Ellie, when Mama and Papa took us to the cathedral in London to witness Cousin Althea's wedding?"

"Yes," her sister said, "but I have never seen a wedding at St. Swithin's before."

The Marchands were regulars at the Sunday services at the seventeenth-century church, as were Kate's grandparents and Kate when she stayed with them.

Prince showed an interest in the unfamiliar people, his back stiff and ears alert. Jane had an arm around the dog's neck. "It's a wedding, Prince," she said to him.

Daniel smiled at her. "Prince has never seen so many people in one place before," he said.

"Miss Bennett got a letter from her sister about a wedding," Elinor said. "Her sister, whose name is Cynthia, is going to be married in June."

"I know," Jane cut in. "Miss Bennett said June was the best month to be married. Why do you suppose that is, Miss Hamilton?"

Daniel's eyes danced and his mouth curved into a grin. "I want to hear this," he said.

Kate wrinkled her nose at him, but put on her governess's voice for the twins. "From a practical point of view, June does appear to be an ideal month for a wedding. The weather is usually neither too hot nor too cold. Moreover, all sorts of flowers are in bloom. Roses, for instance, are at their best. Lilacs are still lovely, too."

Elinor leaned her forearms on the back of Kate's seat. "I think that I would like to be married in a London cathedral one day."

Jane sat forward in her seat and took her arm from around Prince's neck. "I would like to be married in June in a cathedral," she said, doing her sister one better. "Wouldn't you, Miss Hamilton?"

Daniel's gaze connected with Kate's, and she sensed a crucial change in him. Although she looked away, she felt his eyes still on her. She sensed that her reply, for some reason, was of great interest to him.

And, for some unclear reason of her own, she felt compelled to answer. "I think a ceremony in a country church like St. Swithin's would suit me far better than a great splash in a London cathedral. While a wedding should not be a shabby affair, of course, I think, it should be a celebration, not a spectacle."

The twins must have been startled speechless by her revelation, for they sat back in their seats without comment.

Kate felt a little foolish. She had said too much, for Daniel had a silly grin on his face.

"I think it's safe to go now," he said, still smiling as he moved the restive horse onto the road.

The silence that followed ended when Elinor abruptly uttered, "Cook says that she pities the lady Uncle Percy marries. He is a womanizer, which is a man who likes the ladies a little too much."

Kate jerked around and assailed Elinor. "I thought I made it clear that you were not to repeat malicious gossip!"

Elinor's small face became a thundercloud of indignation. "You let Uncle Percy kiss you yesterday on the beach," she blurted out.

Kate's heart constricted. She felt Daniel stiffen by her side. As she turned to face front, she saw the muscles in his jaw go taut.

Kate felt the hot blood rise in her face. How could she have believed that the twins were too naive to make something of Lord Percy's lips trailing down her cheek?

Her humiliation mounted when Jane wailed, "Oooh, Ellie, you broke your promise to Uncle Percy. You vowed that you would not tell anyone that he took Miss Hamilton in his arms."

Jane had added fuel to the fire. But Kate knew she would exacerbate the incident if she continued to scold.

Miraculously, Jane's righteous recrimination did what Kate could not do; it shamed Elinor into a guilty silence.

Kate wanted Daniel to know the truth of the innocent kiss which to her mind was not a kiss at all. He must not think that she was some sort of bold female or believe that she was setting her cap for Lord Percy.

Kate longed to set him straight immediately, but she could not utter an exonerating word as long as Elinor and Jane could hear her.

* * *

In the backseat, the twins had been giggling for some time when Daniel drove off the road onto a primitive track. The chaise bumped down the dirt lane. Laughing, the twins pretended to be thrown all over the seat.

Kate clung to the sideboard and looked over at Daniel. He was smiling. "We are nearly at the lake. A few more yards."

Even before the words had left his mouth, the trees parted and he pulled up into a clearing of cropped meadow grass.

Kate was able to shake off her tension, for Elinor no longer carried an injured expression, and Daniel seemed his amiable self again.

Prince jumped to the ground, trotted to the lake's edge, and slaked his thirst by lapping up the cool water.

Rosie Marr, the widow lady who worked for Daniel, had packed a hamper for their picnic. Kate made sandwiches with the rye bread and ham slices and handed them around and poured lemonade into glasses for everyone.

The rest of the containers of finger foods had been laid out on a tablecloth. They all sat around the edges on the grass and helped themselves to the condiments and wiped their hands and mouths on the linen napkins.

Offshore a cormorant dove into the lake after a fish.

"Did you know that in Japan," Daniel said, "a fisherman ties a line around the bird's leg and uses it to catch fish?"

"Don't the cormorants eat the fish?" Elinor asked. She took a sip of lemonade.

Daniel shook his head. "The fisherman places a ring around the cormorant's neck to make it impossible for the bird to swallow the fish. After the fisherman has all the fish he wants, he removes the ring and lets the bird eat its fill."

"That would be a fine manner in which to go fishing," Jane said. "Far superior to using a rod and reel." She chewed on a carrot stick and gave a little self-induced shudder. "Ugh! I have always found it nasty when Uncle

Percy wrestles a hook from a fishie's mouth and the blood spills out."

Kate thought that a shadow crossed Daniel's face when Jane mentioned her uncle. She was still determined to let Daniel know that Lord Percy's kiss was purely accidental.

Kate fed scraps of ham to Prince and listened to Elinor's determination to catch a cormorant and make the bird into a fisher. Jane got caught up in her sister's enthusiasm.

Kate held her tongue, rather than spoil their fun by throwing cold water on the impractical scheme.

Daniel watched the twins race down to the lake.

"You should have let them borrow the salt shaker," he said, sounding serious.

"Salt shaker?" Kate frowned.

He laughed. "Isn't there some old wives tale about catching birds by sprinkling salt on their tails? I am afraid that our little hunters are doomed to failure."

Kate gave him a feeble smile, repacked the hamper, fastened the leather straps, and carried it to the chaise, where she stowed it on the floor under the driver's seat. When she turned around, Daniel was standing beside her.

"You may rip up at me for what I am going to say," he warned, "but I intend to say it anyway. Just because Percy Westcott is handsome, charming, and wellborn, Kate, does not mean that he is honorable."

Her lip quivered. "The kiss was nothing, a mere accidental brush of his lips on my cheek."

She rushed ahead, describing the episode on the beach that Elinor had precipitated.

"Lord Percy apologized. He viewed it as lighthearted fun and meant no disrespect."

"Fustian," Daniel said harshly. "Percy is a master at wrapping his transgressions in clean linen. He promises to mend his manners to get out of the suds, then, he does whatever he deuce well pleases. He tormented poor Miss Bennett. Addison made every effort to get him to stay away from her, but he could not control him."

"Why not?" Kate still could not believe that Lord Percy was malicious. "If he was such a bounder, Lord Marchand should have found a way to rein him in."

Daniel sighed. "Look, Kate, it is easy for you to say. Addison cannot bar him from the house. Lady Marchand is very fond of her baby brother and views Percy's misdeeds as high-spirited high jinks. To her, he is no worse than most London dandies."

"Maybe he isn't. Did Miss Bennett make charges against him?"

"Nothing specific, just some vague accusations," he admitted. "Naturally, Percy denied any impropriety. Addison wasn't about to make spies of his children by questioning the twins to get at the truth."

"I heard that she was called home to nurse a sick parent," Kate said.

"So she claimed. I just know that Addison received a polite request from her father to let her come home."

Kate saw that Elinor and Jane had given up in their attempts to catch a cormorant and were picking wildflowers beside the lake. Her eyes went to Prince, who lay under a leafy bush, his black nose between his paws.

"Did Lord Percy intentionally befriend Mrs. Morgan to get her to sell him her lake house?"

"You know about that?" Daniel said, sounding surprised. "There is no doubt that Percy wanted the lake house, after all he bought it. Hannah says he badgered her to sell, a moot point, since her rheumatism made her removal to the home for the aged inevitable. His offer, however, was ridiculously low. I wasn't ready to buy at that time, but I made Percy think I was. He panicked and paid Hannah a premium."

Daniel's version was different from Lord Percy's. But a story always had two sides. And who knew for sure if Miss Bennett's parent was really ill? Lord Percy might not be a saint, but neither was he a villain. Kate felt that she was a good judge of character and decided to trust her own feelings and not condemn him on the hearsay of others.

Daniel led Kate to where the chaise shielded them from the twins' view.

"I am tired of talking about Percy," he said. "Let's switch topics."

"To what?"

Daniel put his hands around Kate's waist and lowered his lips over hers in a gentle, noninvasive kiss.

Her hands went around his neck. His mouth was achingly sweet. Kate felt warm and pleasantly shivery in his embrace.

She kissed him back before he lifted his lips and looked down at her.

"There is a vast difference between real love and temporary infatuation," he said softly, but the twins calling Kate's name intruded curtly on the spell he had cast.

Kate came to her senses and stepped from his arms.

"You should not be flirting with me, Daniel, when I am looking after the children," she chided, although she was as much at fault as he was.

"I am not flirting, Kate. My intentions are serious."

She walked from his side to where the twins could see her. Daniel had let her go, and she could see him already tending to the horse.

"Oh, there you are, Miss Hamilton," Jane said, running up to her. "Ellie and I picked these flowers for you." She handed her a bouquet of buttercups that had already begun to wilt.

"Thank you, girls, they are lovely," Kate said, including Elinor in a three-way hug.

Daniel did not say much on the ride home, but Kate did not mind. She had a lot to think about. She welcomed the rhythmic rumble of the vehicle's wheels on the pavement as a backdrop to her thoughts.

I am not flirting. My intentions are serious. Kate had

never had a romance. Daniel's words were as close to a proposal as she had ever had.

Some women might be frightened to be her age and unwed, but she was not. Daniel's kiss had certainly sent her pulses racing. But she did not intend to marry any man unless she loved him without reservations, and she was not at all sure that she loved Daniel in that way.

Seven

Kate was putting the dishes away in the cupboard after supper one cold blustery evening a week later. The wind coming across the lake had been bitter, and Daniel, who had been invited to supper, sat with her grandparents beside the fire in the parlor, having decided to forgo walking the dogs after the meal.

Kate was thinking of his words, *I am not flirting, Kate. My intentions are serious,* as she had many times all week as she put the meat platter in its place on the wooden shelf.

Daniel had never spoken the words again, and while Kate had convinced herself that she was not sorry since she still did not know what her answer would be if he actually proposed in form, she felt a sense of disappointment that he had not made any more romantic overtures like his wonderful kiss.

She was hanging up her apron when she heard a knock on the door. Penny dashed to the top of the stairs and began to bark sharply.

Daniel rose from his chair and said, "I'll answer it;" he shushed the dog and bounded down the steps.

Kate leaned over the upstairs bannister and watched Daniel open the door and felt the blast of chilly air that he let in.

She could hear him and the caller speaking, but could not make out their words. He closed the door and took the stairs two at a time.

"Who was it?" Kate asked, while Joseph and Cloris

looked over the back of their fireside chairs from the other side of the room.

"Royce, the footman from the main house," Daniel said to Kate. "Addison received word that his father has been in a carriage accident. He and Ida are leaving for London and would like you to come at once to stay with the twins while they are gone."

Kate hesitated only a moment before she said, "I will pack a few things," and went to her bedroom.

She threw a nightgown and robe, slippers, and a change of underwear, along with some toiletries into a valise and went back into the parlor, where the others were speculating about the accident.

"It must be serious for Lord Marchand to want to rush off into the night, especially with bad weather expected, instead of waiting until morning," Joseph surmised. "There have been squalls on the coast and those storms usually come this way."

Daniel agreed and smiled at Cloris and said, "As usual, thank you for a fine dinner, Mrs. Cloris," with his customary politeness. "I shall walk Kate over to the main house."

"Dress warmly, dear," Cloris said.

Kate promised she would and kissed her grandmother and grandfather good night.

She went back across the room to where Daniel was already in his heavy coat and was holding her hooded woolen cape for her. He helped her on with the warm garment. She tied the ribbons while Daniel picked up the valise from the floor where Kate had set it down.

"Send word if you get news of the earl's condition," Joseph called after them.

"I shall," Kate said and followed Daniel down the stairs.

Spakes, the butler, opened the front door to admit Kate and Daniel and looked past them into the night.

"I see it has begun to rain," he observed before he shut the door.

"Yes, we got a bit wet," Daniel said as he and Kate divested themselves of their outer garments in the vestibule stacked with portmanteaux and bandboxes. "The wind has picked up even more in the last hour."

"Let me have those, sir," Spakes said and indicated he would take the garments to the kitchen to dry.

Looking solemn, Elinor and Jane came down the stairs in their flowered robes and soft leather slippers, followed by their parents, who were dressed for traveling.

While Lord Marchand and Daniel stepped aside to talk in undertones, Lady Marchand said to Kate, "I would not have disturbed you, Miss Hamilton, but the girls are overset by our sudden departure."

Kate smiled at the children and said all the right things to their mother.

Royce and another young footmen appeared and snatched up the luggage and carried the bags to the traveling coach that was parked in front of the house.

"Sit over there out of the way, girls," Lady Marchand said to Elinor and Jane, who moved at her direction to the visitors' bench beside a potted palm. Kate went over to them, for the mute children's blue eyes were wide and worried.

Elinor and Jane moved apart to let Kate sit between them. She put her arms around their small shoulders and said a few comforting words to them, for she could see how apprehensive they were because of the emergency.

Lord Marchand was talking to Daniel and to Spakes, who had come back from the kitchen, and now manned the door.

"Kiss the children, my dear," the viscount said to his wife. "I want to be in London before midnight."

Elinor and Jane got up from the bench and held out their arms to their mother, who kissed each child's cheek in turn, gave Kate a few last-minute instructions, and followed her husband to the waiting carriage.

Kate took the twins upstairs to their bedroom and tucked them into their beds. "You don't have to stay with us, Miss Hamilton," Elinor said. "Mama just leaves the light by the door burning until we fall asleep."

"Are you sure?" Kate said, although both girls seemed resigned to their parents' departure.

"Janie and I are just going to talk for a while, but we are old enough to stay by ourselves," Elinor assured Kate.

"All right," Kate said. "I am just going downstairs for a few minutes to say good night to Mr. Nealy." She left the door ajar between their chamber and the adjoining bedroom, which had been assigned to her.

Kate joined Daniel in the drawing room, where he stood before the windows that overlooked the lake. He slipped an arm around her waist and pulled her close to him. She tipped her head against his shoulder as, together, they watched the raindrops splash onto the lake and spread into concentric circles. An eerie glow imbued the darkness, making the vista strangely luminous under the black sky. Far off in the distance, Kate saw a flash of lightning.

The butler came to the door and cleared his throat to let them know that he was there. Startled, Kate flinched.

Mr. Spakes asked if there was anything he could get them.

Daniel looked down at Kate, but she shook her head.

"No, thank you, Spakes," Daniel said, "I shall be leaving in a few minutes, and Miss Hamilton will ring if she needs anything."

"Very good, Mr. Nealy. I shall bring your coat from the

kitchen and hang it in the hall," he said courteously and left the room.

Kate took a step from Daniel's side. Her hand went to her cheek as she looked up into his face. "Oh, dear!" she lamented. "What he must think."

Daniel chuckled softly. "Spakes is an excellent butler. Believe me, he has already put it from his mind that my arm was around your waist if that is what concerns you."

Daniel lifted Kate's chin with a finger. "More to the point, my dear, is what you think."

Kate looked up at him, not knowing how to answer; he was such a good man . . . but . . .

A seemingly endless moment passed as he gazed into her face before he said, "Ah, Kate," her name a sigh on his lips. "Still unsure."

Kate lowered her eyes. He wanted a sign that she accepted his proposal. She was loath to let him down, but she could not bring herself to answer yes.

Daniel raised her hands to his lips and kissed one and then the other. "It is all right, sweeting, just be careful. He has no scruples."

Kate blinked. She knew exactly whom he meant, but she was surprised that he thought she had romantic feelings for Lord Percy.

Daniel let go of her hands. "I had better go before the skies open up in truth." The small, sad smile on his face as he said, "Good night, Kate," spoke volumes. He really believed that she fancied Lord Percy.

Kate heard Daniel exchange a few words with Spakes just before the front door opened and closed. She should have denied that she had any romantic interest in Lord Percy Westcott, but it had all happened so fast. It seemed that she had been struck dumb.

Yet, she knew as sure as she knew her own name that she did not love Lord Percy. Daniel would come to see that in time.

But once again, he had warned her that the young dandy had no scruples. To be careful of him.

Was she experiencing some sort of arrested development that she had found fun in the handsome gentleman's childish behavior? Lord Percy was shameless, at times, but he did not offend her. Why was everyone so against him? Kate shrugged. She saw no harm in him. He may be thoughtless, but he was certainly not evilly intentioned.

Eight

After looking in on the sleeping children, Kate pulled on a lawn nightgown, its low neckline trimmed in blue ribbons and Chantilly lace. Outside of her bedroom window the rain lashed against the panes while the wind shook the eaves.

Not yet sleepy, she bundled herself into her warm robe and curled up into a commodious gentleman's chair beside a cheerful fire and opened the Minerva novel that had been left on the bedside table.

She had read only two pages when rolling thunder and flashes of lightning intruded on her concentration. Her heart lurched when an ear-splitting crash rattled the window and sparks spiraled up the fireplace chimney.

Kate's hand flew to her breast. She jumped up and dropped the book into the chair's seat and pushed her bare feet into her velvet slippers and ran to the children's room, certain that the deafening boom had awakened the girls. But to her intense relief, Elinor and Jane slept on soundly, oblivious to the wicked storm brewing beyond their window.

Back in her bedroom, Kate picked up a candlestick that was covered by a glass chimney, went into the hall, and crept down the stairs to the drawing room, where she placed the light on a table beside the door.

To get a better view of the storm, Kate stood at the windows that overlooked the lake, where she had watched the rain earlier with Daniel.

Her breath came hard when lightning zigzagged through the black sky. She was stunned to see that the normally serene lake was an ocean of whitecaps. Waves lapped onto the shore, flooding the beach. Although it was frightening, it was also rather fascinating.

Mesmerized by the way Lord Marchand's precious sailboat rode high in the water as the wild winds tore at its bowline, Kate was not aware that she was not alone and gasped when a male voice spoke her name from behind her.

Turning quickly, she swallowed a cry.

"What are you doing here?"

Lord Percy flashed her a brash smile. "I left the village tavern under a few raindrops, " he said, "but when I got a quarter mile from there, the skies opened up in a furious deluge, and the road became awash in mud. Addison's barn was the first place I came across where my skittish horse and I could take refuge."

He looked down at his ruffled shirt and limp cravat. "I wore a heavy overcoat which became soaked through, so even my dress coat beneath became damp from the torrential downpour."

Kate pulled the top of her thick robe together tightly at the neck as he explained to her that from the barn he had seen a light in the kitchen window and had run to the back door and knocked.

"Cook and Lucy, the scullery maid, were inside drinking tea. Little Lucy let me in and is drying my clothes on a rack by the fire," he said, laughing as though he had just gone through a great adventure.

Kate was too unsettled at being in the presence of a gentleman in her nightclothes to be amused.

"I must get back to the children," she said, in a gracelessly abrupt parting.

As she passed around him, Lord Percy touched her arm. Although she detected a whiff of ale, he did not appear foxed.

"Stay," he pleaded. "Keep me company."

Kate shook her head. "I am in my nightclothes, my lord."

He chuckled. "You are more chastely bundled than if you were dressed in a ball gown."

He was sparring with her, for he knew that was not the point, but she said, "I am not dressed for receiving a gentleman."

"I'll overlook it," he said, but Kate ignored him and walked at a brisk pace toward the door.

"Wait, Miss Hamilton, Kate, I would have a word with you." His melodious voice had become urgent. "Please, it is important to me."

Important? Frankly curious, Kate stopped and turned around.

Lord Percy's face softened into a shy smile. "I am quite besotted with you, my dearest Kate," he almost whispered, "and I would make you mine if you are willing."

Kate was flabbergasted. Was he joking? Had she heard right?

He came to her side. "I command considerable wealth, you know," he said persuasively. "I own a town house in London where you would be mistress with servants to do your every bidding. I would shower you with jewels and send you to the best dressmaker in the City."

He held his breath, like an adolescent, Kate thought, who was afraid that the girl whom he desired might turn him down.

Her heart went out to him. She could not accept his proposal, of course, but neither could she hurt his feelings by turning him down too quickly. Buying time, Kate said, "We hardly know one another, my lord."

His importune proposal was flattering. Yet, she could not marry him, for not only did she not love him, but in her heart she knew that he was poor husband material.

His plaintive eyes pleaded.

Trying to be kind, she said, "Marriage is a serious undertaking, my lord."

His face fell. "Marriage?" His cheeks reddened.

"No, no, Kate. You misunderstand. Don't you see? I like you, but I can never marry you. I have to look higher than the daughter of a knighted nobody. Why, your grandfather is a common laborer. Good Lord, my marquess father would be appalled if I took someone of your inferior station to wife."

Kate paled. What he was offering her was not marriage, but a *carte blanche!* What a fool she had been.

He looked more than a little irritated when she backed away from him.

"Come, come, Kate, be sensible. What I am offering you can be better than marriage. You don't want to be a governess all your life. I am openhanded when it comes to my mistresses. Each of them has left the liaison richer than when she entered it."

Kate felt her color rising. She had defended this libertine to Daniel. How could she have been so wrong? Shame flooded her.

But saving pride quickly returned. "You had better leave, my lord," she said in a firm voice, her head held high.

One fair eyebrow slanted upward. "I guess that means your answer is no. You were quick enough to encourage me when the twins were around to protect your virtue," he scoffed.

Kate looked at him with cold contempt, but said nothing.

He shrugged, walked past her, and left.

Kate stood at the window for a long time. The sound of thunder came from a great distance now and the flashes of lightning were no longer visible. Rain still fell, but the violent storm had been brief and had already blown itself out.

Kate wanted to cry. She had played games with Lord

Percy while all the while Daniel waited patiently. She was truly loved, and she had resisted. Lord Percy was a rogue, but she was not blameless. She had encouraged him. Would things have been different if she had been more experienced with men? Or was he so handsome that he could make a naive female believe anything?

Her brown study came to an abrupt halt when Kate became aware that someone was pounding the brass knocker on the front door rather vigorously. She went into the vestibule, but Spakes was nowhere in sight.

"Who is it?" she called through the oak panels.

"Daniel," came the answer. Her heart quickened as she pushed back the bolt, opened the door wider, and stepped aside to let him in.

Kate had all she could do to keep from throwing herself into Daniel's arms. His wonderful face was stamped with strength and character. How could she have not seen the difference between him and Lord Percy?

He closed the door, pulled off his gloves, and pushed them into the deep pocket of his coat.

"Why are you downstairs in your nightclothes, Kate?" he asked, sounding mildly inquisitive, but not critical.

"The noise of the storm kept me awake," she said, biting her lip.

He looked surprised when tears welled in Kate's eyes.

"Upon my soul, sweeting, the storm has frightened you. Take heart, it has passed."

She wiped her swimming eyes with the back of her hand. "Why are you here?"

He brushed the hair from her cheek. "I promised Addison I would keep an eye on you and the twins. I decided to check back before I retired for the night to see that all . . . was as it . . . should be." His voice faded.

Kate looked up at him. His face had become a dark cloud as he stared over the top of her head.

"What is it, Daniel?" she asked and turned around to see what had caused his black mood.

Kate gasped.

Lord Percy was coming down the hall, wearing a paisley dressing gown and carrying a brandy snifter in his hands.

He sat down on the visitors' bench and nonchalantly warmed the cognac between his palms.

"Daniel," he said with a polished smile.

"What is he doing here?" Daniel growled.

Kate was shocked; she worked to keep her tone level, but was unsuccessful.

"Lord Percy was caught in the storm and took shelter here," she croaked.

Daniel let out a brittle laugh. "He lives less than three minutes away. The storm has been over for some time."

"I wish you two would stop talking about me as if I could not answer for myself," Lord Percy said, swirling the cognac in his glass and sniffing the potent liquid's aroma. He winked at Kate. "I would think our attire would give you a hint, Daniel, as to our purpose, but my lips are sealed. A gentleman never reveals a lady's indiscretions."

Kate turned around and faced Daniel and saw that he looked ready to kill Percy.

"Daniel, please don't hurt him," she pleaded, her concern for Daniel not Percy. She put a hand to Daniel's chest to get his attention.

He pushed her hand aside and took a step toward Lord Percy. Kate begged, "No, please, please. Nothing happened. He is lying."

But Daniel was not looking at her, not listening. He was furious. It frightened Kate. Lord Percy was just the sort to bring charges with the local magistrate. Daniel's friendship with Lord Marchand would be damaged irreparably if he thrashed Lady Marchand's pampered brother. All this was partly her fault. She had to stop Daniel.

Kate stood firm before him. He would have to lift her

bodily to get to the dandy. "Don't, Daniel. Don't. I cannot let you hit him."

His eyes were darkly suspicious as he stared down toward Kate's chest. Her hand touched the lace at the top of her breasts where her robe had fallen open. Quickly, she snatched the robe back together, hiding her nightgown, but Daniel had already shot her a look of pure disgust.

"I seem to be dripping all over Lord Marchand's floor," he said, unemotionally, opened the door, and left, slamming the door behind him.

"Daniel, wait," Kate cried, but by the time she looked outside, he was already gone.

Kate trembled so badly that her hands shook. She rounded on Lord Percy. "You are despicable!"

"No need to ring a peal, Kate. It was all a joke. Look," he said. He stood up and let loose the dressing gown belt; the silky robe fell open. Kate was startled to see that he was fully dressed underneath.

"I grabbed Addison's robe from the laundry room after I heard Daniel's voice." He burst out laughing. "Lud, the look on his face was absolutely priceless. It was too funny for words." He laughed harder and harder.

Kate had an urge to slap his care-for-nobody's face senseless. "I should have let Daniel plant a facer and rearrange your pretty face."

Lord Percy wiped his streaming eyes. His glee sagged a little.

"My, such bloodlust," he said, mocking her. "I can see it would have been a mistake to take you as my mistress. In any case, I don't know what I was thinking. I like my bedmates young and showy. You never would have lasted a week under my protection."

Lord Percy gave her a wicked smirk and turned around and walked back toward the kitchen. What a contemptible human being he was!

Later in bed, sleep would not come for hours to Kate. Somehow she had to find the words to appeal to Daniel's good sense and make him understand that she had been protecting him, not Lord Percy. Her last thought before she finally fell asleep was that it would be unbearable to lose this rare man whom she had finally come to realize she loved.

Nine

Lord Percy's traveling carriage rolled by, the boot
packed with expensive luggage, as Kate and the twins
watched from the front steps in the morning sun, the air
clear and fresh after the storm.

"Seems Uncle Percy is going to London," Elinor said.

Good, Kate thought and wished that he would stay there
forever as the coach vanished around the bend in the lane.
But, of course, that was not going to happen. Lord Percy
Westcott was destined to be a constant living reminder to her
of her own gullibility. But she had something much more
important on her mind this morning than wanton dandies.

Elinor and Jane ran ahead of Kate up the hill toward her
grandparents' house. She had told the twins that she
wanted to see how the Franklins had come through the
storm, but her real motive was to find Daniel and to try to
repair their relationship, if he would only listen.

A farmworker hurled broken branches into a wagon bed
while another raked up the fallen leaves and twigs which
littered the lawn between the carriage house and Daniel's
cottage.

Joseph dragged the branch of an oak tree from Daniel's
yard, lifted the limb into the wagon bed, and then walked
over to meet Kate and the children.

"Good morning, Grandpa," Kate said. "It looks as if you
had quite a bit of damage to your trees."

"Some, but, thankfully, all of the buildings remained
intact," he said, and turned to the twins and doffed his

black cap to them. "Greetings, Lady Elinor and Lady Jane," he said, rendering them a courtly bow that made the girls giggle.

"Well, now, ladies," he said, "did you think the world was coming to an end when you heard that roaring thunder and saw those bolts of lightning last night?"

Elinor pulled a face. "Janie and I slept right through it. I think Miss Hamilton should have woken us up, don't you, Mr. Franklin? Everyone is talking about the storm, and we missed the whole thing."

"Most unfair," Joseph commiserated. His countenance remained suitably grave, but his gray eyes twinkled.

Kate looked over at Daniel's cottage, where Prince was getting up from his nap and stretching out his hind legs.

"Do you know if Daniel Nealy is at home, Grandpa?" she asked.

"No, he's not, Katie. Some sort of sickness has broken out among Lord Herford's flock," Joseph said. "Daniel was sent for last night to treat the sheep and might be gone until tomorrow."

Prince came over to Joseph's side and the old man laid his hand on the dog's black head.

"Daniel left a note tacked to my door, asking me to look after his two cats and Prince. Can I help?" he asked.

Kate gave him a swift smile. "No, it will keep. I'll just go now and visit with Grandma."

Leaving Joseph to his chore, Kate walked toward the carriage house, feeling upset and let down. Her carefully rehearsed speech would have to be postponed. Daniel had been terribly angry and openly disgusted with her. She worried that he would not believe her, not forgive her. The waiting and wondering was hard on her nerves.

She opened the carriage house door and Elinor and Jane climbed up the steps in front of her, using the handrail.

Cloris helped the children from their coats and listened to Elinor complain about sleeping through the storm.

"I agree, ladies, Miss Hamilton should have awakened you," she said with an impish tilt to her lips.

Kate rolled her eyes. "Sure, I should have, Grandma," she said dryly and hung her cape on the rack beside the stairwell.

"Come into the kitchen, children, and see what I have for you," Cloris said and led them into the cozy room, where delectable aromas of fresh baked goods permeated the air.

She sat Elinor and Jane down at the well-used kitchen table and gave them each a warm apple tart from the dozen on a tray on the sideboard.

"Kate?" she asked, offering her a tart.

"No thank you, Grandma," Kate said and took two mugs from the cupboard and poured milk into them from the pitcher on the table.

After setting the mugs in front of Elinor and Jane, Kate went to the window and looked down into the yard. "The petunias we planted were beaten down by the rain," she said.

Cloris came to stand beside her and perused the little garden. "Hmm," she mused. "I imagine the flowers will revive in a few days. Plants have a way of doing that." She moved closer to Kate. "Come into the parlor," she said in a near whisper.

Kate glanced at the twins, who were eating their pastries and talking with one another.

"Elinor and Jane will be fine," Cloris said in an undertone and nudged Kate toward the kitchen door.

In the parlor, Kate sat down on the comfortable old sofa and Cloris sat down beside her. "What is this about, Grandma?" Kate asked.

"What happened at the main house last night?"

Kate feigned innocence. "Happened?"

"Katie, don't even try to fob me off. Lucy came to fetch their ration of milk this morning and she had a lot to say."

"Then, it might be better if you told me what Lucy said."

Cloris looked impatient, but said, "All right."

Kate stared at the Bible on the sofa table, a little apprehensive,

"According to Lucy," Cloris said, sounding a bit dramatic, "Lord Percy was riding home from the village tavern and was caught in the storm and got soaked. He sought shelter in the main house and left some clothing in the kitchen to dry and went into one of the public rooms to wait for the storm to pass." She paused, but Kate was determined not to be helpful.

"Sometime later, Lucy and Cook heard raised voices, Daniel's and Lord Percy's and yours. The two women did not dare to interfere, but Cook did rouse Mr. Spakes, who had retired for the night. But before Mr. Spakes could investigate, Lord Percy came back into the kitchen, retrieved his clothes, and went home. Mr. Spakes went to the front of the house, but Daniel had left, and you had gone to bed."

Kate had expected to hear much worse. Her being alone with Lord Percy had gone unnoticed. Her own pride would not allow her to disclose his insulting proposal to her grandmother, or anyone else for that matter. That secret would go with her to her grave. She was mortified to realize that she had unwittingly given Lord Percy enough ammunition for him to believe that she would become his mistress.

Cloris curled her wrinkled fingers around Kate's cool hand.

"It is said that Miss Bennett left her post because of Lord Percy's attentions," she said. "Has he behaved improperly toward you? Is that what he and Daniel were quarreling about? Was Daniel protecting you?"

If only! Kate thought and chose to quibble. "Grandma, Lord Percy harbors old animosities toward Daniel. And Daniel does not like him by half. Lord Percy poses no danger to me. And, no, Daniel was not protecting me from him."

Nothing would have been served by describing Lord Percy's charade to her grandmother.

Kate began to rise from the sofa, but Cloris said, "Wait." Kate feared a cross-examination was coming.

But Cloris's worry lines smoothed as she said, "I went with your mother, my Charlotte, one long-ago summer to visit the Roman ruins across the lake as everyone hereabouts was doing. Matthew, your father, and his assistants were a nine-days' wonder, for we country folk knew nothing of archeologists. Your father came to supper a few days later, for he and Charlotte had become friends. You know, I was sure from their first meeting that Matthew was destined to be her one true love. I have a sixth sense about these things."

Kate had been vaguely aware that her parents had met at the Roman ruins across the lake. "No one ever told me the details, Grandma. You make it sound very romantic."

"It was, but I tell you this about your mother," Cloris said, "because from the day Daniel brought Penny's medicine over when we were restoring the garden, I have sensed that he is the man who will truly love and cherish you."

"Yes, I know, he is," Kate murmured.

Cloris appeared dumbfounded.

"Don't look so shocked, Grandma. Did you think I would miss seeing Daniel Nealy's worth?"

Cloris uttered a bark of skeptical laughter. " Frankly, yes. But I am happy that you have proven me wrong."

"We had a fight," Kate said sadly.

"All lovers quarrel," Cloris replied. "You'll make it up."

"Elinor! Jane!" Kate called.

She pulled her cape across her shoulders and helped the girls into their pink coats.

Kate melted into her grandmother's comforting hug. The kindliness she felt in Cloris's embrace made Kate's eyes tear.

"I want him, " she whispered as Cloris caressed her back.

But it was sheer torture to be forced to worry that Daniel might not want *her* anymore.

Ten

Kate washed up after a long, miserable day. Never before had she spent so much time thinking about one person. Never before had someone mattered so much to her. Time and again, she had felt like crying, agonizing over the possibility that Daniel might spurn her.

She had patted her face dry and had placed the towel back above the washstand when there was knock on the bedroom door.

"One minute, please," she called, pulled her robe over her chemise, and went to the door.

Mr. Spakes stood in the hallway under a dim light.

"Mr. Nealy is here, Miss Hamilton. I have put him in the drawing room."

Hope leaped into Kate's breast. "Thank you, Mr. Spakes," she said. "I will be right down."

She took off her robe and shook out the blue sprigged muslin that she had tossed onto the bed a few minutes before and pulled the dress back over her head. Her fingers trembled as she hurried to fasten the pearl buttons on the bodice.

Kate felt flushed and her nerves were on edge as she left the room. She paused in the doorway to the drawing room, where Mr. Spakes had fired up the wall sconces and had put a match to the coals in the fireplace. The days were longer now, and while there was still some fading light outdoors, the rooms were already dark.

Daniel leaned against the windowsill, his back to the lake.

He cast Kate a polite smile and came forward. She noticed that his black coat was dirty.

"Spakes gave me the good news that Addison sent word from London that the earl does not have life-threatening injuries and is on the mend."

"Yes," Kate said. "Lord and Lady Marchand are returning the day after tomorrow." She covered the few steps between them and looked up into his face.

Daniel looked awfully tired, and he smelled of animal. He rubbed the back of his neck.

"I had to quarantine some twenty afflicted sheep, but the rest of the flock should survive. I know that I should have gone home and cleaned up, but I feared I would be tempted to lie down to rest and would sleep round the clock," he said apologetically. He sighed wearily. "I have not been able to stop thinking about Percy and you and last night. I want to put the matter to rest once and for all before it drives me crazy."

Kate was unsure whether his remarks were ominous or favorable. But he looked so exhausted that she was moved to say, "Please sit down, Daniel."

He shook his head. "If I crumple into a chair, I won't have the energy to get up. I have not slept since I saw you last."

Daniel ran his large hand through his dark hair. "Once I regained my senses, I realized that Percy had deliberately cast you in a bad light. I never should have doubted you, Kate."

Kate's spirits lifted. "Lord Percy tricked both of us, Daniel. He was fully dressed beneath a dressing gown that he had confiscated from Lord Marchand's laundry."

Daniel grimaced. "I know. Long afterwards, it came to me that Percy had his boots on. Damme," he said, "I never should have let him get the better of me. If you had not curbed my jealous rage, I might have smashed my fist into his face. When a man is in love, he tends to act irrationally."

Joy washed away Kate's misgivings. *When a man is in love* was all that registered in her brain.

Instantly everything was wonderful. She was heart whole again. "You do love me," she said.

He laughed. "Kate, my sweet, have you not been paying attention all these weeks?"

Kate's happy giggle was cut off when she found herself in his arms and his lips on hers in a series of hungry, possessive kisses. Her heart beat overtime. Against her breasts, Daniel's heart was pounding as wildly as hers. The reality of romance staggered Kate's emotions. His kisses were hard and fierce and deep and experienced.

When Daniel lifted his lips from her bruised mouth, her knees were weak. He held her close to him and stroked her back and gentled her in a long silence that said more of his love than words.

Cupping her shoulders, he looked down at her, his expression earnest. "I want us to be married, soon, very soon. I will speak to your grandfather."

Kate smiled up at him. "You shall have no trouble there. Both Grandpa and Grandma respect and admire you." Her own expression sobered. Lord Percy had found her social standing unacceptable. She did not want to go there, but still she said, "What of your parents, Daniel? You are a baron's son and I . . ."

He put a finger across her lips. "Shh, Kate. My parents love me. In my family, a child's happiness always comes before social duty 'else I would never have been encouraged to follow my inclinations to be a veterinarian. But do you think for a minute that if my father said nay to our marriage, I would concur? I am my own man, my darling," he said without the slightest artifice. She had to believe him.

"Now," he said, "there is but the when and where to settle."

"The banns must be called," Kate reminded him.

"All right. That will take us into June, which should suit

you fine, if I am not mistaken. Did you not say to the twins that June is an ideal month for a wedding?"

"Yes, and given your excellent memory you probably recall that I want to be married at St. Swithin's in the village."

"Done," Daniel said. Kate thought it was a marvelous thing that he was so accommodating.

"We will even have a place to live," he said. "Lord Wiggens's lake house finally went up for sale. My agent informed me yesterday that the baron accepted my bid. The timing could not be more propitious."

He had mentioned the property before and Kate knew it was in the pines directly across the lake.

"Oh, Daniel, how splendid," she said. "The house is perfectly lovely."

"I am glad that you are pleased." He gave her a light kiss. "I should like nothing better than to kiss you nonstop until dawn, but I must take to my bed. Let us meet at the carriage house tomorrow at noon, and we can finalize the wedding plans with your grandparents."

The weather cooperated magnificently for Kate and Daniel's wedding. The June day was warm and sunny with only the lightest breeze coming across the lake. Daniel's cheerful family was much taken with Kate and had put her grandparents completely at ease within moments of meeting them.

The nave of St. Swithin's Church was pleasantly scented with a profusion of white and purple lilacs.

Cloris sat in a place of honor in a front pew, dressed in a rose crepe fit for a duchess. The baron and baroness were across the aisle from her. Daniel's two brothers, three sisters, their spouses, and their children filled three rows in the little church. Lord and Lady Marchand and Elinor and Jane sat directly behind Cloris. Every pew was crowded with the lake people, the villagers, and the workers from the estate.

Kate was radiant in a pale lavender silk gown trimmed lavishly in exquisite Brussels lace. She walked down the aisle on the arm of her grandfather to the mellow sound of the old organ. Proud in a new black suit similar to the groom's, Joseph put Kate's hand into Daniel's and patted the shoulder of his happily weeping wife as he sat down beside her to hear the Anglican priest read the age-old vows.

Later the newlyweds stood on the stone steps outside the church doors. Atop the steeple the gold cross gleamed in the sunlight.

Daniel pressed Kate's arm close to his side in sweet possession. Happiness overwhelmed her. She got up on her toes and kissed him full on the lips.

"You are the joy of my heart," she whispered.

"And, you, my sweet, as your grandmother would say, will always be my one true love," he answered. "My only love, my beloved wife."

THE HUSBAND HUNT

Kate Huntington

This book is dedicated with love to my parents, Max and Mary Saluke Hoch, of Huntington, Indiana, who were married on June 12, 1948. Happy Anniversary!

One

May 1, 1814
London

Everard Montclair, the Earl of Stoke, had always known his brother Michael was a fool.

Soon the whole world would know as well—at least, as much of the world that mattered.

Everard supposed it would take a heart of stone to remain unmoved by the tearful countenance of his pretty sister-in-law, a lady of whose existence he had remained ignorant until his brother solicitously ushered her delicate, trembling form into his study and stood with his arm around her, looking every inch the protective hero in his regimentals as Everard watched this touching demonstration of devotion with a jaundiced eye.

Hero.

What a joke.

If Lieutenant Michael Montclair truly had been the hero he impersonated, he would have told Everard about his marriage to a foreign bride of respectable but undistinguished lineage in private. But Michael was too cowardly to face his elder brother's wrath like a man. Instead, he subjected his child-bride to it, no doubt in the belief that Everard would not give him the reprimand he so richly deserved before this innocent witness.

In that, Michael was mistaken.

"Had it slipped your memory," Everard said awfully, "that you are engaged to marry Lady Linnea next month?"

Michael's chin was up, but his upper lip was dotted with perspiration. He couldn't quite meet his brother's eyes.

"That was a marriage arranged by our families," he said. "You cannot expect me to honor that."

"Obviously not," Everard said dryly, "since to do so would be to condone bigamy. How could you serve Lady Linnea such a trick? To do so is the act of a blackguard."

Michael's ears turned pink on the tips.

He could not meet Everard's eyes. Instead he looked at his bride, whose tear-stained face was made no less beautiful by her distress.

"When I met Vittoria, I could think of nothing else," he said softly. "To marry another would have been . . . unthinkable."

I have boots older than this girl, Everard thought in disgust.

"I hardly expect *you* to understand what it is to be in love," Michael said defensively.

Everard could not believe his brother would say such a thing to him. He felt his face turn to stone.

Michael seemed to realize what he had said at the same time, and he gave Everard a look of genuine contrition.

"Forgive me, Ev," he said, hanging his head, "I do not know what possessed me—"

"It happened a long time ago," Everard snapped, "and it is nothing to do with the subject at hand."

Indeed, it had been so long since her death that sometimes Everard could no longer see his beautiful, golden-haired Elizabeth's face clearly in his imagination. She was still there, though, in his mind and in his heart. She always would be. It was to his everlasting regret that he had not returned from war soon enough to make her his wife before he lost her. Instead, he learned of his fiancée's death in a letter. He would never forget the pain that had lanced through him when he read the terrible words.

"I will write to her today," Michael said.

"No!" Everard's hands balled into fists so tight they left his knuckles white. No one should ever have to receive such news in a letter. Michael might claim his match with Lady Linnea was one of convenience, but the severing of it was certain to bring her world crashing to a halt, just as Elizabeth's death did his. "You must see her in person. It is the only decent thing to do."

Michael looked into his young bride's dark eyes.

"I could not leave Vittoria here, among strangers, and I could hardly take her with me on such an errand. So, it will have to be a letter," Michael concluded with a shrug.

The coward.

The truth is, he is afraid to face the woman he has led on for six years and then jilted, Everard thought scornfully.

It would not be so bad if Lady Linnea were still possessed of a rich dowry and the expectation of a reasonably good inheritance from her father. Such a young lady, though disappointed and embarrassed, could simply look for another husband.

Unfortunately, Lady Linnea's family had received a reversal in fortune due to her father's insatiable penchant for gambling. In fact, she had been living in straitened circumstances with her father for some time in the country, and the only thing that kept her father's creditors from descending upon his manor house to confiscate all their portable possessions was Lady Linnea's impending marriage to a young officer whose elder brother was one of the nation's richest peers.

Now, it seemed, Lady Linnea had been scorned by the fiancé who was to be her salvation.

And, as was usual upon such occasions, it would be up to Everard, as head of his family, to make it right.

Only the presence of the still-quaking Vittoria kept Everard from giving his brother a tongue-lashing he would never forget.

The girl looked up at Michael through her long, velvety eyelashes as if he personally had hung the sun in the sky.

Her hero.

Ah, well. She would learn the painful truth soon enough.

The fact was, polite society tended to look down on foreign brides under any circumstances and was particularly disapproving when the bridegroom in question had jilted one of their own. Such a man could expect to find himself placed far beyond the pale, and his wife would be ignored by society.

Everard had not met Lady Linnea above once or twice, and that was years ago, when he was on leave from his regiment and obliged to attend the chit's come-out ball. It was when his father was still alive and pleased to form a family alliance between one of his sons and the daughter of his good friend, the then-wealthy Earl of Wrenthorpe. Everard remembered Lady Linnea as a shy, dark-haired, solemn little thing, exactly the type of female likely to hero-worship a handsome weakling such as Michael, who had looked so dashing in his yet unbloodied regimentals.

Everard gave his brother, who was cooing to his pretty bride in the most disgusting manner imaginable, a look of utter contempt as he wondered which of Michael's ladies he pitied more.

As usual, it would be up to Everard to repair the damage done by the thoughtlessness of one of his many dependents. Indeed, over the years since his father died and he had stepped into his shoes as the head of the family, Everard had become quite adept at such matters. It took him only a moment to formulate a sensible plan to compensate Lady Linnea for her inconvenience.

"Since you will not do so, I shall leave at once for Leicestershire," he told Michael and his bride, "after I have spoken with Aunt Augusta."

"What the devil for?" exclaimed Michael, who, like Everard, was not fooled by the still-beautiful widow's fashionable air of fragility. Lady Augusta had a genius for reducing strong men to a state of witless anxiety. And Michael had demonstrated that he was far from strong.

"Aunt Augusta is Lady Linnea's godmother. If you will recall, you met your fiancée at a ball in her house."

"Do not call her that! She is *not* my fiancée!" snapped Michael, visibly shaken by the prospect of a dressing-down by his formidable aunt. "I owe her *nothing.*"

"I feel quite certain Aunt Augusta would disagree with you."

Indeed, when her favorite nephew called on her later in the afternoon in order to acquaint her with Lady Linnea's plight, that fashionable lady had plenty to say about Michael's lack of chivalry toward Lady Linnea.

"The poor child!" his aunt cried. "She will be devastated! Michael should be horsewhipped! And to bring a foreign bride home with him as a *fait accompli!* I hope the woman is presentable, at least."

"You need have no concern on that score. The young lady seems quite refined. I am going to Leicestershire to see Lady Linnea," Everard said grimly. "I do not relish the task of telling her that Michael has married another woman."

Lady Augusta turned relieved eyes on her nephew.

"I am so glad you did not mean for it to be me," she admitted. "You know I always say the wrong things to people."

"I quite understand," he said wryly. "She most probably will go into strong hysterics—"

"Not she," Lady Augusta interrupted. "Linnea is a sensible girl."

Privately, Everard doubted any young lady could receive such bad news without raising the roof with her wails, but he let it pass.

"I cannot leave Lady Linnea in the country to fend for herself among her father's creditors. Nor can I take her to my town house with Michael and his wife in residence. It would not be proper, anyway, since mine is a bachelor household. May I bring her to you? I thought perhaps you could take her to Bath or some other watering hole and live quietly with her until the scandal blows over."

"You may depend upon me, dear Everard," she said. "I will spare no exertion to be of comfort to the poor girl, even though I have many commitments in the city during the Season. However, I can hardly think of my own pleasure when my poor, disappointed goddaughter so desperately needs cheering up."

She quite spoiled the effect of this altruistic sentiment by adding with a little frown while looking up at her nephew through artfully darkened lashes, "Or, at least, I *hope* I may contrive to entertain Linnea suitably, but the thing is I am compelled to be the least bit cucumberish until next quarter day—"

"You may leave that to me," said Everard, who knew his pretty, extravagant aunt was perpetually outrunning the constable. He frequently found himself obliged to render her assistance in settling her debts, even though the jointure left her by her late husband was universally considered to be quite handsome.

It was a great imposition for Everard to be saddled with the responsibility for yet another purse-pinched female, but he could well afford to support Lady Linnea for the present. Never would he allow anyone to say he had failed in his duty to the wretched girl.

"Darling Everard," Lady Augusta said warmly.

Everard took his leave to instruct his valet to pack for a journey into the country. He invited Mrs. Phoebe Montclair, one of his dependent female cousins, to go with him, for it would not do to risk damage to Lady Linnea's reputation by traveling with her unchaperoned.

Everard would have preferred to escort the coach on horseback in such fine weather, but he knew the occasion, in addition to good manners toward his cousin, demanded that he maintain his dignity by riding inside. He could hardly arrive on Lady Linnea's doorstep to deliver tidings of such a delicate nature in a muddied condition and smelling of horse.

"Cousin Everard," his cousin said hesitantly, breaking into his grim thoughts.

Her expression was anxious. He smiled at her.

"What is it, Cousin Phoebe?" he asked. It wasn't *her* fault that his brother was a thoughtless pig.

"What are we to do with the poor girl once we fetch her? It would be extremely awkward to bring her to your town house with Cousin Michael and his new bride in residence."

Extremely awkward. Now, there was an understatement.

"I have arranged for Aunt Augusta to escort her to Bath. Bath can be quite dull, but there is certain to be a bit of a scandal, and she would be more comfortable in quiet surroundings until it blows over."

"Bath! Oh, the fortunate girl," Mrs. Montclair said wistfully. "I know it is dreadful of me, but I so miss going about in society."

It was on the tip of Everard's tongue to suggest that Mrs. Montclair make one of the party to Bath, but he knew Aunt Augusta would object. The two ladies rather disliked one another, although Cousin Phoebe, at least, had the good manners not to show it.

Everard patted her hand.

"Not dreadful at all, my dear cousin, but only natural. Your period of half-mourning will soon be over, will it not? We must have some new gowns in colors made for you. I shall arrange a theater party, so that you may show them off."

Cousin Phoebe's late husband was another of Everard's connections who had made no provision for his dependents, and so left his wife's welfare in Everard's capable hands. He was, in fact, the benefactor of a great number of such dependent ladies.

"How excessively kind," she said, dimpling with pleasure. "You have so many matters demanding your attention. I did not expect you to think of my needs at such a time."

"It is my very great pleasure," he said, and it was true.

He always had been very fond of Cousin Phoebe, possibly because she was one of the few of his dependents who actually seemed grateful for his assistance. The others merely accepted it as their due.

"Papa, how *could* you!" cried Lady Linnea in despair when her father proudly showed her the many bottles of vintage wine he had bought, supposedly for a song, from a neighbor. They were standing on the doorstep where a burly carter had deposited the dusty bottles.

"Tut, tut, Linnea. Berkland is an old friend. He is willing enough to wait for payment until you have tied the knot with young Montclair," the old gentleman assured her.

To her dismay, her father had been borrowing against this expectation for some time, for, he was quick to point out, it would hardly do for Lord Stoke let his brother's father-in-law be taken to Fleet Street Prison for nonpayment of debt.

Which, to Linnea's mind, was all the more reason for her father to curb his extravagance. She recalled the present Lord Stoke as a proud, rather magnificent man with compelling green eyes and rich chestnut hair who had quite terrified her when she was a girl just out of the schoolroom.

"Young Montclair should be home soon, should he not, my dear?" the earl asked in the mistaken belief that bringing up the subject of Linnea's approaching nuptials would distract her from his extravagance.

"I expect him any day," Linnea said, smiling, even though she wasn't sure how she felt about her impending marriage. She had not seen Michael for several years, although she had written to him every week since their betrothal.

He had written to her less often, but that was understandable. A soldier had far more demands upon his time than a young lady living in impecunious circumstances in the country. Still, he had been a regular correspondent, more or less, and the fact that she had not received a letter from him in several months filled her with foreboding.

The war with Napoleon was over. Why did he not come home?

Her father, normally not the most intuitive of creatures, patted her hand.

"I am certain young Michael will present himself, hale and hearty, on our doorstep in good time," he said.

"The wedding is only seven weeks away," Linnea could not stop herself from saying. The wedding had already been postponed three times due to the demands of Michael's military career. She feared her bridal gown, made years ago, was sadly out-of-date, but it would have to do.

"And a grand one it will be. Your Michael is a lucky lad, for there isn't a finer girl in all the kingdom than you."

Linnea smiled at him.

Her father was irresponsible, extravagant, outrageous, childlike, selfish, and, in general, a great source of worry to her. But the love he had for his only child was never in dispute.

"You worry too much," her father said. It never occurred to him that Linnea could afford to worry less if he would stop careering over the countryside, searching out new sources of vintage wine they could ill afford for him to purchase. She knew from long experience that pointing this out would only hurt his feelings. "Why do you not have a cup of tea?"

"Perhaps I will," she said, smiling, even though the tea box was empty and had been for several weeks.

"Good girl. Do not worry about this lot," he said, grandly indicating the wine that the carter had deposited inside the front entrance of the house. "I'll see to it."

"Thank you, Father," she said with a sigh as her father went off to find their aged butler, who would help him stow the wine in the cellar. Despite her father's strenuous objections, Linnea had been forced to discharge her maid, his valet, and most of the other servants long ago.

She was about to go into the house herself when she saw a traveling coach lurch drunkenly up the rutted drive. She shaded her eyes against the sun and gave a sharp intake of breath when she saw the crest on the door.

It was the Earl of Stoke's crest.

Her heart started beating erratically.

Could it be Michael, at last?

To her dismay, the handsome, grim-faced gentleman who alighted from the carriage was not her fiancé, but the formidable earl himself. He was wearing a somber black coat and hat.

She could think of only one reason why he would come to her in such state.

Her heart had nearly stopped, but she straightened her shoulders and waited for him to come to her.

"Good morning, my lord," she said gravely. "How kind of you to pay us a visit."

"Good morning, Lady Linnea," he said, removing his hat. "I must speak with you privately on a most urgent matter."

"Of course," Linnea said, biting her lip to keep it from trembling. "Do come in, my lord."

Two

Lady Linnea, Everard noted with approval, was much improved from the shy girl she had been at eighteen. Her curly dark hair was simply arranged, her figure was slight, and her once-fashionable blue gown was decidedly shabby, but she carried herself proudly. The Earl of Wrenthrope's manor house had fallen into sad neglect, but his daughter offered its hospitality as if she were a queen. She no longer was rendered tongue-tied in his presence, which was a relief.

"May I offer you some refreshment, my lord?" she asked as she seated herself upon the sofa and indicated that he was to take the armchair opposite. Instead, he seated himself next to her. He could hardly shout such tidings from across the room. Her face paled a little.

"No, I thank you. Lady Linnea, you must forgive me. I see no gentle way to impart the news I bear."

She bowed her head, but before she did, he saw the quick sheen of tears in her eyes.

"It is as I feared, then, when I did not receive any letters from him in reply to mine," she said softly. "I thank you, my lord, for taking the trouble of bringing me this news in person when you must be even more grievously saddened by your brother's death than I. Has the funeral taken place? If not, I should like to attend."

Her concern, incredibly, seemed to be for *him*.

As he hastened to reassure her that his brother yet lived, he reflected that regardless of how sympathetic she seemed at the moment, she might well wish Michael dead before this day's work was done.

"My dear Lady Linnea, I assure you my brother is quite well."

She blinked at him in surprise.

"Then, why—"

"He is married," he said bluntly.

"Married," she repeated. She sat back rather abruptly and stared straight ahead with a slightly unfocused gaze. "To someone else. I see."

"He met her in the Peninsula," he went on, relieved that she apparently was not going to make a scene, even now that she knew the worst of it. "I knew nothing of this until he brought his bride to my house in town straight from the ship that brought him to England, I assure you."

"I see," she said again.

He began to think a torrent of tears and recriminations might be preferable to this deadly calm.

"I am prepared to offer you compensation—"

She turned clear, intelligent eyes upon him. Her hands trembled slightly, and her jaw was clenched. He could see that despite her semblance of poise, she was very, very angry.

"For your inconvenience," he continued doggedly.

"Do go on, my lord," she said with a bitter smile. "I am eager to learn what compensation you consider appropriate for this humiliation. The church has been reserved. The invitations have gone to the post. The formal betrothal announcement appeared in the newspapers long ago. My bridal gown resides in my wardrobe sheathed in muslin."

Well, that surprised him. Everard had half expected her to reject his offer of compensation out of hand from sheer pride. Of course, he would have insisted. She could ill afford such scruples with a father such as hers. But he was glad she chose to dispense with the usual female nonsense of hysterics and fainting fits that a lesser woman might have indulged in at being spurned by her betrothed husband.

He always had admired practicality in a woman.

"I understand completely, and you will not find me ungenerous," he said briskly. "I have made arrangements to send you with Lady Augusta, your godmother, to Bath, where you may live down the scandal quietly. At my expense, of course. I will also arrange for a dowry, so that you may marry respectably if the time comes that you wish to do so. If you would be good enough to instruct your maid to pack a bag for you, I should like to get on the road at once. You need not bring much. I shall provide whatever else you require."

Lord Stoke's complacent expression told a resentful Linnea that he expected her to sink to his feet in a puddle of gratitude now.

Instead, she itched to wipe the condescending smile off his face.

Patronize *her*, would he?

"What earthly good," she demanded, "will it do to send me to Bath?"

"Or any resort of your choosing, of course," Lord Stoke said smoothly. "Do you have friends at one of the others? Tunbridge Wells, perhaps, or Scarborough?"

"Hardly! But a quiet watering hole populated by invalids and octogenarians seeking a cure for their ailments while the London social Season is in full swing and all the eligible men are elsewhere will hardly answer my purpose."

"Your . . . purpose?" he asked hesitantly. "I do not understand."

"Of finding a husband, of course," she said with upraised eyebrows. "And without delay."

"A husband? But I thought—naturally I thought after your very natural disappointment, you would wish to retire quietly for a time to recover."

"My dear Lord Stoke, for one who enjoys a reputation of such acuity, you are proving remarkably unperceptive. My expectation of marrying Michael is the only thing that has held my father's creditors at bay thus far. Once his debt of honor was paid from his personal fortune, there was nothing left but this house and the unentailed property. He has been living—and spending—on the expectation that my marriage to Michael would take place ever since."

"I know this, of course," Lord Stoke said, nettled. "That is why I am prepared to bestow a dowry upon you. Your father may be subjected to his creditors' feeding frenzy with my goodwill, for he richly deserves it. You do not."

"Think, my lord. What do you suppose will happen to this dowry once it leaves your hands?"

"It will come under your father's control," he said slowly.

"Precisely," she said with grim approval. "He would be on the way to London and the gaming tables with your bank draft in his hand before the ink was dry on it."

"And there is not a thing you or I can do about it," Lord Stoke acknowledged.

"Not a thing," she agreed. "So, as much as I appreciate your generosity in the matter of this proposed excursion to Bath, it will not do. According to the agreement between your father and mine, I am promised a husband on June 19, and I am afraid that only a wedding on June 19 will do. St. Paul's is already reserved. As your father's heir, you naturally will have inherited this obligation along with his other honors."

"My good girl, surely you do not expect—"

"I expect you to provide me with a husband as a substitute for the one of which I have been deprived."

"A husband," he repeated blankly.

"I am abundantly aware that they do not grow on trees," she acknowledged.

"How . . . reasonable of you. And where am I to find such a person on such short notice?" he asked dryly.

"Well, that is the heart of the matter, is it not? I believe your other brothers are married."

"As you well know, Michael is the youngest."

"A pity. And have you any eligible male cousins?"

"None of a suitable age," he said with an involuntary smile that was almost . . . charming. "So, where does that leave us?"

He had the gall to look amused.

"That leaves *you* with the task of finding me a husband. Any gentleman of appropriate age or station who is capable of controlling my father's extravagance will do," Linnea told him. "I assure you that I do not intend to be too choosy."

"You relieve my mind," he said dryly. "And if I fail?"

"I shall have *you*, of course," she said. "Unless you and your brother would prefer to endure a suit for breach of promise. *That* should make the scandalmongers happy. And I would win, of course."

The look on his lordship's face was priceless. Linnea could have found it hard to keep from laughing if her heart were not in grave danger of breaking.

"So I thought," she said coolly when he seemed to have no answer to her outrageous proposal. Now that she had shaken him out of his insufferable sense of complacency, she relented. "Do not look so horrified, my lord. I thank you for taking the trouble to pay this visit to me, but I assure you that I expect nothing more of you."

"But you should," he said calmly, "for as you so rightly pointed out, as head of Michael's family it is my responsibility to see that you suffer no injury for his failure to fulfill his promise of marriage to you."

"Lord Stoke," she said in dismay, "I spoke in anger and in haste. You have discharged your obligation, and I thank you for it. Nothing more is required."

"Nonsense, Lady Linnea," he said, looking stubborn. "I insist."

Three

Everard settled in the forward seat of his carriage oppo-site Lady Linnea and his cousin with a sigh of satisfaction.

The girl had argued until she was blue in the face, but once her father joined the fray, she had no choice. She was a stubborn little baggage, but at least she had enough decorum not to disobey a direct order from her father, unsatisfactory as that gentleman might be as a parent.

Far from being loath to accept Everard's assistance, the Earl of Wrenthorpe was indignant to learn that Everard had no intention of making a financial settlement on his daughter. Lady Linnea had made Everard see the futility of *that,* at least. Lord Wrenthorpe was so annoyed that he did not insist upon accompanying them.

Everard would have nipped *that* idea in the bud at once—the old reprobate *deserved* to stay alone in the country and sulk—but it would have wasted precious time in further argument, and he had far too many obligations in London to spend more than one night on the road.

Dusk had arrived by the time they stopped for the night.

"I will arrange for our rooms," he said when they ar-rived at a bustling inn. "You will wait here."

Linnea frowned at him when he exited the coach. It obvi-ously did not occur to him that either of his companions would fail to obey his command, Linnea thought crossly. The arrogant Earl of Stoke was far too accustomed to getting his own way. His cavalier treatment of Linnea's father had bor-dered on contempt. Linnea knew she should be grateful to him for his willingness to right the great wrong his brother had done her, but she was finding it very, very difficult.

"Is he not wonderful?" Mrs. Montclair said with a sigh. "A Season in London! You fortunate girl! Bath would have been very pleasant, but *nothing* is to compare with London! How you shall enjoy it."

"I am certain I shall," Linnea replied civilly enough. It was hardly Mrs. Montclair's fault that one of her cousins was a high-handed autocrat and the other was a faithless blackguard.

"I am out of half-mourning next week, and Cousin Everard said I am to have some new gowns made in colors," Mrs. Montclair went on. "Such a considerate man. He thinks of everything."

New clothes. The Earl of Wrenthorpe's formerly spoiled daughter, who once purchased her gowns from the most expensive dressmakers' shops in London without a thought to their cost, seemed a stranger to Linnea now.

Linnea thought of the outmoded clothes in the battered trunk securely strapped to the roof of the coach.

Well, they would have to do a bit longer.

"Do not worry," Mrs. Montclair said, for all the world as if she could read Linnea's mind. "Cousin Everard does nothing by half measures. You will have a new wardrobe, too. And a handsome husband before the cat can lick her ear, mark my word."

Linnea smiled weakly. Now that she had spent several hours in close confinement with his royal haughtiness, she shuddered at the memory of her brass-faced boldness in telling him that she would have him as husband if he could find her no other.

How could she have done such a thing?

London, for heaven's sake! Exactly where she might expect to find Michael and the happy bride.

But it was no use condemning Lord Stoke for his meddling.

She had no one to blame for this odd turn of events

except herself. Someday she *must* learn to control her impulsiveness!

Linnea tried to convince herself, to no avail, that the ultimate humiliation would be having Lord Stoke to thank for the very clothes on her back. She had spent the past few years telling herself that modish gowns were fripperies, and she could do very well without them. But the small, pathetic voice inside her heart that was starved for pretty things gave a sigh of smug satisfaction.

She was such a hypocrite, she admitted to herself.

The prospect of spending the night at a comfortable inn was heaven to a woman who had spent the last few years in a drafty, crumbling mansion with virtually no servants left. Neither she nor her father had a taste for living in the country, so the house had been sadly neglected. Not in a million years had they thought that someday they would be reduced to living on his entailed property. If they had, they might have seen to keeping it in better repair. Unfortunately, after he lost his fortune they were financially unable to rectify the matter.

Linnea so hoped her father would not buy too much vintage wine or too many horses while she was not there to keep an eye on him. The Earl of Wrenthorpe prided himself on driving a hard bargain every bit as much as he prided himself on his ability to win at cards—and with results just as disastrous. Nothing Linnea said to him would ever convince the earl that buying wine and horses at bargain prices is *not* an economy when one hasn't the funds to pay the piper. Her father was well liked in the neighborhood, and otherwise sensible persons did not hesitate in the least to extend credit to him.

The more fools they, except it was Linnea whose stomach knotted at the thought of how much debt her father had incurred on the strength of his expectation that Linnea was to marry the younger brother of a very wealthy man. And that was *before* Michael jilted her.

Jilted her.

Her mind tried to wrap itself around the enormity of this outrage, but it couldn't, really.

"I wonder what she is like."

"I beg your pardon, Lady Linnea?" Mrs. Montclair asked politely.

Had she voiced that thought out loud?

"I was thinking of Michael's . . . wife."

Mrs. Montclair gave her a look of great sympathy.

"It will not do to dwell on such things," she said softly.

Linnea gathered that the bride must be very, very beautiful.

"I am merely curious," Linnea said with a creditable show of indifference. "She is Spanish, I assume?"

"Yes. A small woman with dark hair and dark eyes." Mrs. Montclair eyed Linnea speculatively. "In fact, Lady Linnea, she is much in your own style although not quite so pretty, if you do not mind my making such a personal observation."

The corners of Linnea's mouth formed a smile of their own volition.

"I do not mind," she said. "Not at all."

Mrs. Montclair blinked, as if in surprise.

"You have such a lovely smile," Mrs. Montclair said. "Truly, I do not know what Cousin Michael was thinking of."

Perhaps Mrs. Montclair's remark was merely a kind lie, but Linnea was inexplicably cheered by it.

Vanity, she thought, *thy name is Linnea.*

"I had never seen Cousin Everard so put out! He gave Michael a tremendous scold on your behalf, I promise you." She gave a rapturous sigh and smiled brightly at Linnea. "And now you are going to London instead of stuffy old Bath. How delightful."

"Yes. London," Linnea said, willing her stomach to cease its nervous churning.

The coach door opened abruptly.

"Come along, then," the Earl of Stoke said as he extended

one strong, gloved hand to Mrs. Montclair. "Dinner is bespoken in a private parlor. I hope you will not mind sharing a bedchamber. The inn is rather crowded at this season."

Linnea blinked at him like a ninny. She had assumed she would share a room with the earl's cousin, for it would be criminal to incur the expense of a room just for her.

"Of course, one of you could have my bedchamber," he said, apparently misunderstanding the reason for her silence, "and I will sleep in the taproom or the stable. I did so often enough in my army days."

"What utter nonsense!" Linnea exclaimed. "Why should you? I do not mind sharing if Mrs. Montclair does not."

It was Everard's turn to be surprised.

With the exception of Cousin Phoebe, the ladies of his family took it for granted that Everard's mission in life was to ensure their comfort, and few of them, he felt sure, would have any qualms about relegating him to the stable under such circumstances. Unfortunately, few of them got along with the others.

Of course, Lady Linnea was not a member of his family. He supposed that self-indulgent father of hers spared little thought for her welfare.

"Dear Cousin Everard," Mrs. Montclair said. "Always so gallant!"

Everard smiled at his cousin and assisted her from the coach. When he turned to perform the same office for Lady Linnea, he found that she had already alighted on her own.

"You did say dinner was bespoken, did you not, my lord?" she asked. "I find I am quite famished."

A half hour later, it was with some difficulty that Everard kept a straight face when he helped Lady Linnea to a second serving of potatoes to go with an enormous portion of the rare roast sirloin he had ordered for himself.

He was glad the sirloin had been a large one, or he might not have got any.

"Will you have some sauce with that, Lady Linnea?" he asked.

"Thank you, yes," she replied.

Mrs. Montclair, it was apparent, did not know how to look in the teeth of Lady Linnea's gluttony. The young lady ate neatly, and her table manners were everything one might expect of an earl's daughter, but it was clear that the quantity of foodstuffs she consumed shocked the widow very much.

Lady Linnea was such a little thing. Where was she putting it all?

Apparently sensing Everard's thought, Lady Linnea looked up from her plate and saw that Mrs. Montclair and Everard both had finished their meal and were regarding her with astonishment.

"Oh, dear. I have done it again," she said with a rueful smile. Her eyes sparkled with mischief, and Everard began to see what had attracted Michael to the girl in the first place. "I am afraid I am not one of those frail flowers who waste away to nothing when they are nervous."

"Evidently not," the earl said dryly. *"Are* you nervous, Lady Linnea?"

"Well, yes, actually," she said thoughtfully. "My future is so uncertain. But I feel much better after that wonderful meal." She gave a luxurious sigh. "Now that I have been fortified, I can face anything."

"I am glad," he said, deciding that Lady Linnea certainly was easy enough to please. For himself, he did not consider the food anything special.

Mrs. Montclair, seeing that Lady Linnea had at last put down her fork, began to rise as a signal to the younger lady that it was time for them to retire to their room so that Everard could enjoy a glass of port or whatever beverage he preferred in solitary masculine state.

"Is there not a sweet?" Lady Linnea asked, looking a bit disappointed.

Everard, who had expected to be saddled with a spurned little tragedy queen all the way to town, thanked the

Almighty that Lady Linnea apparently had not one whit of feminine sensibility.

A healthy appetite he could deal with.

"Give me a moment," he said, rising to find a waiter.

Good manners dictated that Lady Linnea beg her kind host not to put himself out on her account.

"A piece of cake, perhaps," Lady Linnea suggested instead. "Or some berries in cream. Or pie. I am excessively fond of pie."

"So am I," Everard said, grinning at her as he winked at his astonished cousin and left the room in search of sustenance for his protégée.

"Lady Linnea, are you quite well?" Mrs. Montclair asked anxiously. "You are not going to be ill, are you?"

"No," Linnea said absently as she looked at the door through which her benefactor had disappeared.

That unexpectedly boyish smile of his quite took her breath away.

Linnea shook her head in an attempt to clear it.

She had endured a terrible shock. It was plain that she was not thinking clearly.

"Are you quite sure?" Mrs. Montclair persisted.

"Quite sure about what?" Linnea asked.

"That you are all right. Your complexion looks rather flushed."

"Oh, certainly," Linnea said, smiling for the elder lady's benefit. "I am perfectly well, I assure you."

A good night's sleep, she told herself firmly, and the Earl of Stoke would revert to the haughty, self-important meddler Michael's letters and her own experience years ago had reputed him to be.

"Cherry pie! My favorite!" she cried when the gentleman returned to the room with a servant who set the pastry on the table with a flourish and then left at the earl's gesture of dismissal.

"Lord Stoke, I think I will marry you after all," she said jokingly as she inhaled the sweet aroma of the still-warm pie.

Then Linnea's face flushed with embarrassment. How *could* she have said such a silly thing?

To her relief, he only laughed.

"If only all the ladies were so easily pleased," he murmured. "May I help you to a slice, Cousin Phoebe?"

Linnea thought it was quite charming the way he deferred to the elder lady in concession to her age. Many men would not have been so considerate of a middle-aged poor relation.

"A very small one," that lady said, sounding a bit smug. No doubt she was proud of her exquisitely small appetite.

Lord Stoke smilingly complied.

Without her asking, he cut a large piece for Linnea and then one for himself. A twinkle lurked in his eyes.

Euphoria, Linnea told herself rather desperately.

The pie—and only the pie—was responsible for her sudden attraction to a man who had barged into her life, sneered at her father, and took her off to London without so much as a by-your-leave.

Of course, she *liked* London, although she had been at pains to deny this to her father, who felt bad enough about having to sell the town house and move them to the country.

These unwelcome feelings she had for the Earl of Stoke could be attributed to her greedy appetite, nothing more. She was *not* going to make a fool of herself over Michael's insufferably proud brother!

"Cousin Everard is so kind and handsome," Mrs. Montclair said carefully after she and Linnea had been escorted to their comfortable room by their benefactor. "He is most probably the most eligible bachelor in London."

"I have no doubt," Linnea said stonily.

"Ladies often mistake his exquisite manners and generosity for something more serious," Mrs. Montclair persisted, "when it is not. And it is very hard for him to bring himself to repulse them. I think I do not speak entirely from my natural prejudice toward a gentleman who has been extremely kind to me in my widowhood when I say that Cousin Everard could have the richest, most beautiful young lady in the kingdom to wife, if he chose. A royal princess would not be too good for him. I say this for your own good, my dear Lady Linnea."

Such a gentleman would hardly wish to settle for *her*, Mrs. Montclair meant to say.

"I understand, but your warning is quite unnecessary. I assure you, I have no designs on Lord Stoke."

"That is all right then," Mrs. Montclair said, looking relieved. "I just knew you were a sensible young lady. I beg your pardon if I have seemed impertinent."

"Not at all," Linnea said, forcing a smile to her lips in order to reassure the lady.

When Mrs. Montclair would have said more, Linnea gave a prodigious yawn.

"I feel sure you are as weary as I am," she said. "Let us retire. I suspect your cousin is one of those dreadful persons who awaken bright-eyed and full of vigor, and will want to be on the road by dawn."

Four

Fortunately for the state of Linnea's vulnerable heart, Lord Stoke reverted to his usual overbearing self the next day over the breakfast cups in the private parlor he had procured for their use. The coach awaited them outside in preparation for the last leg of their journey to London.

"You expect *me* to attend a ball at your house in honor of Michael's marriage?" she asked in disbelief.

And to think she had been entertaining tender feelings for this man. She must have been mad!

"Nothing would answer the purpose better," he said in a tone of voice that suggested that *she* was the unreasonable one. "It would make an excellent impression upon society. The gossipmongers will be quelled at once if they see that the ending of your betrothal to him was perfectly amicable."

"Perfectly amicable! How can you *say* such a thing! He jilted me practically at the altar. I wrote to him for *years*, and like a ninny I prayed every night for his safe deliverance from battle. The wedding was postponed three times while I waited for him to come home from war. He has made a complete fool of me."

"True. But it can hardly do your consequence or his any good to air *that* little Cheltenham tragedy in public!"

"Brilliant," Mrs. Montclair breathed. "Positively brilliant! Dear Lady Linnea, you must see how excellently this will answer."

"Must I?" Linnea said stonily. "Do you have *any* idea how everyone will stare at me?"

"They are going to stare at you, anyway," Lord Stoke said with a careless shrug. "We might as well give them something to look at. Trust me, Lady Linnea. I am thinking only of your own good."

"I think *not*, my lord," she said coldly.

"I beg your pardon," he said with haughtily lifted eyebrows. "To what end do you think I have brought you from the country and engaged myself to finance a Season for you in London at not inconsiderable trouble and, I might add, at not inconsiderable expense, if not to preserve your reputation?"

"I think it is not *my* reputation you are so intent upon preserving but your brother's and his wife's," she said with a huff of annoyance. "And your own, perhaps. I am not ungrateful for your intervention in my affairs. But it is your brother, and not I, who will be put beyond the pale for reneging on our betrothal without you to dress the ugly matter in clean linen. *I* am the injured party, and blameless in this affair. It is *he* who stands to earn society's condemnation, and not I!"

"Perhaps so," Lord Stoke acknowledged, "but it is *you* who stands to earn society's pity at being jilted. Poor, pathetic Lady Linnea, rejected by her fiancé for another woman practically on the eve of their wedding. Is that not worse?"

The thought made her cringe.

"Yes," she admitted through gritted teeth. *Blast him!*

"So, I offer you a way to save face."

"And save Michael's and his wife's while you are at it."

He favored her with a smug smile. He had her, and he knew it.

"Clever, is it not?" he asked.

"Very," she said stonily. "I congratulate you."

"Then you will do it?" he persisted.

"I will do it," she said with a sigh.

"Excellent," he said, although it was plain from his expression that he never had been in doubt of her capitulation.

How it galled her to accept his charity, knowing she was obliged to dance to the tune of his piping.

"First, the shops!" cried Mrs. Montclair as soon as they arrived in London and installed Linnea in Lady Augusta's town house. Unfortunately, Linnea's godmother was not home, but Mrs. Montclair was more than willing to step in as Linnea's chaperon.

The ladies' benefactor smiled indulgently.

"An excellent idea," he said, handing one of his own visiting cards to Mrs. Montclair. "Present this at Miss Lacey's establishment with my compliments, and she will take good care of you. Do not make any effort to economize, Cousin Phoebe, I beg of you. You will be going out into society now that you are out of mourning, and you must have suitable clothing. As for Lady Linnea, we must do our best to present her to her best advantage."

Linnea was never more conscious of the sad state of her gray traveling costume, which once had been the height of fashion, but now was sadly outmoded.

Her lip curled.

Linnea had been living quite out of the world the past few years, but even she knew how unmarried gentlemen came to be such valued customers of London shopkeepers who specialized in ladies' apparel.

"Thank you, my lord," she said coldly, "but I do not wish to be mistaken for one of your mistresses."

He frowned.

"Highly unlikely," he said sardonically as he looked her from head to toe.

Mrs. Montclair fanned herself and looked as if she might faint at such an improper exchange.

"However, I perceive your confusion, and must hasten to reassure you," he continued blandly. "I was responsible for the debuts of several young cousins over the past three years, and I patronized Miss Lacey's establishment on their behalf."

"Of course," Linnea said, aware that in her annoyance

she had committed a solecism of no mean order. No woman of quality would admit that she was aware of the existence of the sisterhood to which she had referred.

Which was absurd, of course. Linnea had no patience with such missishness.

"Dare I ask if you have arranged for Michael's wife to patronize Miss Lacey as well?" she asked.

"No, I have not, Lady Linnea," he said. The man had the gall to look amused. "I have sent her to a different dressmaker in a different street."

"You think of everything," Linnea said.

"I do try," he said modestly. "But perhaps you are weary after your long journey and would prefer to put off your shopping excursion until tomorrow."

"Oh, surely not," cried Mrs. Montclair, looking disappointed.

Linnea, although she regretted the necessity of accepting Lord Stoke's charity, was not enough of a hypocrite to deny that she, too, would be glad for some new clothes.

Had the insufferable man not said they must do their best to present poor, dowdy Lady Linnea to her best advantage?

"I am not at all tired, I assure you," Linnea told Mrs. Montclair. That lady brightened instantly.

"A pair of redoubtable ladies, indeed," Lord Stoke said without a hint of sarcasm. "I shall go home at once and send one of the town carriages so you will have it at your disposal."

"My lord?" Linnea said.

"Yes, Lady Linnea?" his lordship asked with one eyebrow raised.

"Be sure to send a very *large* one," she said sweetly. "I rather think we will have many, many parcels."

"I shall," he assured her. "And I will send a pair of strong footmen along to carry them."

* * *

Lady Augusta was furious with Everard for permitting Mrs. Montclair to take Linnea on her first shopping outing in London instead of waiting for her to do the honors.

"Phoebe Montclair is a complete ninny," she sniffed. "She has been living quite out of the world this last age, and—mark my word—she will trick the girl out like a Christmas goose and introduce her to no one but a parcel of shabby genteel mushrooms."

"My dear Aunt Augusta, you know you have far too many social obligations during the Season to take Lady Linnea shopping. Perhaps you will be kind enough to have a ball for her in the very near future, say, next week? Miss Lacey should have some of her gowns finished by then. I know it is unconscionable of me to expect you to organize a ball on such short notice. Only you could manage to bring it off. It would be more comfortable for Lady Linnea to become reintroduced to London society at a ball in your house instead of at the rather larger one I shall host in Michael and Vittoria's honor."

Augusta's brow smoothed out like magic, and she bent a cajoling look upon him.

"Very true. Well, I *had* planned on having a ball and several dinner parties this Season, but the price of entertaining is *so* dear."

"Let me worry about that," he said, patting her on the hand. "You will have all the bills sent to me, of course. It's the least I can do if you are willing to take Lady Linnea under your wing."

"Of course, I will, Everard," she said. "The poor thing. How humiliated she must be. You did say Michael's bride is presentable?"

This last was said with a penetrating look.

"Quite," he said. "Of a most respectable family in Spain. I think you will be delighted with her manners."

"Thank heaven. I did worry about that. Having a dirty dish in the family is always tiresome."

"I agree. I trust you will do your best to quell any un-kind gossip about my brother's wife as well."

"You may depend on me, Everard," she said, dimpling. "About the party—I envision something rather small and very exclusive with as many suitable men as I can contrive to secure on such short notice."

"Excellent," Everard said. "Now, I must go."

"I will send you an invitation, of course. I depend on you to come."

"A pleasure," Everard said. It was the least he could do, he thought as he bowed and took his leave.

Now that Lady Linnea's future was assured, he could enjoy the luxury of immersing himself in estate matters and forgetting all about her.

Five

It was the evening of Aunt Augusta's ball, and, to Everard's annoyance, he was mistaken about the time and arrived so early that the receiving line was not yet in place.

Everard instructed the butler to show him to the library and not bother his aunt with the news of his arrival.

To his surprise, he found it already occupied by a lady he almost failed to recognize.

When he first had met Lady Linnea years ago, she was a nervous, painfully shy debutante just escaped from the schoolroom who answered his every conversational gambit while they were dancing in painfully self-conscious monosyllables and trod upon his toes. On that occasion, she was dressed in a girlishly demure gown of pale pink muslin that turned her complexion sallow, and her hair was crowned with a wreath of pink and white roses that had started to wilt in the heat of the ballroom.

A week ago in Leicestershire he thought her much improved, but he still regarded the task of getting her a decent husband a challenge.

Now he saw he had greatly underestimated either the lady's charms or the talent of Miss Lacey.

He would send the seamstress a richly deserved gratuity for this.

Lady Linnea's dark hair had been cropped to frame her delicate features in flattering natural curls and give her face an enchanting elfin quality. Her expertly designed

gown of peach-colored silk brocade displayed her slender
figure to advantage and made her lips and skin glow.

She was standing by a bookcase, perusing a book, and
her long, dark lashes cast shadowed velvet half-moons on
her pretty cheeks.

He was about to announce his presence when his aunt's
rather penetrating voice stopped him cold. She burst into
the library from the other door.

"Linnea!" Aunt Augusta scolded. "I could not think of
where you had gone when I sent Simpson to my room for
the rouge pot."

"Simpson may keep her rouge," Lady Linnea said gaily,
turning to Lady Augusta with a teasing smile on her lips.
"I have not stooped to painting my face in all of my five-
and-twenty years, and I am not about to start now."

"Now, you listen to me, girl," Lady Augusta said sternly,
"how can you expect to make a favorable impression on
my nephew if you won't exert yourself the tiniest bit to
show yourself to advantage?"

"I have no objection to being introduced to a bachelor
or two," Linnea said in the same teasing tone. "It is why I
came to London, after all. But toad-eat your conceited
nephew, I will not."

Startled, Everard drew further back into the shadows.
It was ungentlemanly in the extreme for him to listen to
their conversation, but he was only human, and he wanted
to hear what else they would say about him.

"Everard is *not* conceited," Augusta insisted. "He is an
excessively modest man considering the positively *shameless* way every female over twelve fawns over him, but I
tell you, my dear, he has *enormous* influence with the *ton.*"

"Even so, I am strangely reluctant to appeal to the absurd creature's vanity as a solution to my difficulties. Let
us instead place an advertisement in the *Gazette* as I did
for my pug when I could no longer afford to keep her.
'Free to a good home. One mature, domesticated female.
Good bloodlines. Gentle with children.'"

"Very droll," Augusta said, trying not to laugh at this raillery. "I wish you would trust me to know the way of the world a little better than an inexperienced chit who has been buried in the wilds of Leicestershire for the past few years."

"Very well, Godmama," Linnea said, raising both hands in surrender. "What must I do?"

"I want you to make an entrance."

"I beg your pardon?" Linnea asked, pausing in the act of taking another book that had caught her fancy down from the bookshelf. "Do you not want me to receive the guests with you?"

"No. I want you to make an entrance," Augusta repeated, "so all the gentlemen will notice you."

"They will notice me," Linnea said glumly. *"Everyone* will notice me. The gossips will have told everyone by now that Michael has returned from the war with a bride."

"We will say nothing of *that,* if you please," Augusta said. Her lips were a thin line of disapproval. "I told Everard that if *I* were the head of the family, I would have Michael horsewhipped."

"Perhaps he did me a favor," Linnea said with a sigh. "I would rather suffer the mortification of being jilted now than endure the humiliation of having an unfaithful husband later. It is clear that he was not nearly as devoted to me as I was to him."

"Very wise, my dear," Augusta said. "It is fortunate for Michael that he has kept out of my way since his return to London, for I would be delighted to give him a piece of my mind!"

"Pray, don't on my account," Linnea said. "I am well rid of him."

"But the fact is, you need a husband. You are not getting any younger, you know. And so it is of crucial importance for you to make a good impression on my nephew."

"Too late! He has already judged and found me wanting," Linnea said gaily. "But I shall do my best to ingratiate myself with the man."

"Excellent. Everard is invariably late to these affairs, which is often the case with these fashionable gentlemen," Augusta explained kindly for the benefit of her unsophisticated charge, "so you should wait at least a half hour after the receiving line is in place before you come into the room. I want him to appreciate that pretty dress to the fullest."

"All right," Linnea said. "Indeed, I will find the books in your library excellent company until then."

Satisfied, Lady Augusta left the room.

Linnea, her nose in her book, absently started walking back toward the bookcase in front of Everard. He was hidden in shadow, so she didn't see him. Still reading, she was almost close enough to touch him when he decided he had better announce his presence.

"Lady Linnea," he said quietly.

She looked up and nearly dropped the book.

"Lord Stoke!" she gasped.

"I did not mean to startle you," he said stiffly.

"May I ask how long you have been standing there?" she asked. Sudden heat rose to her cheeks.

"Long enough to learn that I am conceited, absurd, vain—did I leave anything out?" he asked with excruciating politeness.

Linnea looked apprehensively at him, then she let her breath out in a long sigh of relief when he laughed at her expression.

"Oh, thank heaven!" she said. "I was afraid I had offended you."

"No. I am too familiar with the way Aunt Augusta's mind works to take offense. How like her to decide that it is time I took a countess and that it might as well be you. I imagine, knowing her idea of subtlety, that you are sick of hearing my name by now."

"Is that what you thought?" she asked. Her eyes were alight with wicked amusement. "Be assured, my lord, that I have no intention of setting my cap at you, nor would the thought of my doing so even enter your aunt's head. You are, if you please, to condescend to exert your influence in order to bring me into fashion—"

"My good girl—" he began severely, strongly suspecting he was being roasted.

"—You having such *enormous* influence with the *ton*," Linnea continued. "One dance with you, and I would be *made*. Gentlemen would be stumbling over their own feet to pay their addresses to me."

"If I ever heard such rubbish!" He was absolutely revolted.

"Do you mean it isn't true?" Her eyes were wide and innocent.

"Good God, no!"

"I should have *known* it was nothing but a take-in," she said. Her crestfallen tone was at odds with the mischief in her eyes. "It will have to be a toothless widower with six children, after all."

He gave a crack of laughter, but privately Everard thought it would be a pity, indeed, if Linnea were to be wasted on a toothless widower.

He glanced at the watch hanging from a fob at his waist.

"I perceive that you may not go to the ballroom for at least a quarter of an hour," he said. "Shall we look for a deck of cards?"

"Good of you, but I hardly think that will be necessary now that you are here," she said. "Perhaps you should go to the ballroom, and I shall come along a bit later. Do contrive to pay attention to my entrance, or you will be in Lady Augusta's black books."

"I shall do my poor best," he said, smiling at her.

Linnea told herself, quite sternly, that positively *slaying* ladies with his smile probably came as naturally to the man as breathing.

He gave her a mocking little bow and left the library. She waited a few minutes to give him time to reach the ballroom well ahead of her, then she emerged from her hiding place.

"Ah, there you are, you naughty girl," Lady Augusta scolded fondly when she saw her. She turned to her nephew with a bright, superficial smile on her face for the benefit of those guests who happened to be watching them. "I was just telling Lord Stoke—you *do* remember Lady Linnea, do you not, Everard?—that I could not imagine where you had got to."

Linnea blinked in astonishment at this blatant falsehood.

Lord Stoke smiled mischievously at her. She could not help smiling back.

"I was unavoidably detained," she said dryly.

"How charming to see you again, Lady Linnea," Lord Stoke said gallantly. "I do hope you mean to make a long visit in town? Perhaps you and Cousin Augusta will go for a ride with me in the park one afternoon."

He was speaking in an unnecessarily loud voice, and Linnea gave him a quelling look which he chose to ignore.

"Our dance, I believe," he continued, which was probably just as well because Linnea found herself bereft of speech.

Lady Augusta smiled approvingly as Lord Stoke drew Linnea toward the circle of waltzing dancers.

"Spreading it on rather too rare and thick, my lord," Linnea said just under her breath.

"Lady Linnea," he said, favoring her with another devastating smile for the benefit of his aunt. "I am shocked to hear such an ungenteel expression on those delectable lips."

"Delectable, are they now?" she said pensively. "That sounds very promising. Are my eyes to be compared with sapphires or merely stars?"

"My good girl, do acquit me of anything so unimaginative. You must think me a slowtop, indeed."

"Merely a fashionable fribble."

"You are too severe."

"Lord Stoke," Linnea said, peering up at him suspiciously. "Are you *flirting* with me?"

"Of course," he said, looking at her in a way that made her heart knock rather painfully against her ribs. Now she knew how the formidable earl became such an object of adoration for the ladies. When he was of a mind to be charming, he was devastating. "Otherwise, how *am* I to bring you into fashion?"

"How kind."

"I am never *that* kind, Lady Linnea."

Her eyes flew to his face and found him gazing at her with such sincerity that she looked down again.

"What a shameless bouncer," she said.

"Worse and worse!" he exclaimed, sounding scandalized. That made her smile.

He was laughing down into her eyes when she looked past his shoulder and saw her father waving cheerfully at her.

"What is it?" Lord Stoke asked.

"Good heavens! It's Papa," she said, swallowing hard.

Oh, dear. Lord Stoke had made it perfectly plain in Leicestershire that his offer of hospitality did *not* extend to her father. Linnea's heart sank. It was clear that her father was far advanced in his cups. And he was dressed in the most peculiar manner. His shirtpoints rose so high that he had to turn his whole head to look to the side. His pantaloons were extremely tight, which did not flatter his plump limbs. With a sinking feeling, Linnea realized that he must have gone even further into debt for the ridiculous clothes that transformed him into an aging coxcomb.

Lord Stoke turned his head and sighed.

"Come along," he said brusquely as he took her hand and strode across the room to confront her father.

"Good evening, Lord Stoke," Lord Wrenthorpe said genially. He looked smug and pleased with himself, as if he had done something very clever, which was always a portent of disaster. Linnea's heart sank. "If you will excuse us, I should like a word with my daughter."

"Of course," Lord Stoke said. He bowed and relinquished

Linnea, but she could see that his lips were compressed in a thin line as he did so. Linnea thanked Providence that Lord Stoke was too well bred to make a scene in his aunt's house, for it was plain that he was angry.

"Papa, what are you doing here?" Linnea said as she caught his arm and led him toward the library and privacy. "I thought we agreed it would be best for you to remain in the country."

"*He* agreed, the pompous young upstart," the earl said rather too loudly for Linnea's peace of mind. She did not make the very grave error of trying to shush him, though. She knew from dealing with her father and other volatile persons in the past that such a course would only make them shout all the louder. She quickened her pace and hoped they would reach the library before he said anything *too* indiscreet.

"Lord Stoke," Linnea said tersely, "has been very generous toward me. He even arranged for me to stay with Lady Augusta so that I would not have to share his roof with Michael and his wife."

"Most proper," her father said with a frown. "He could hardly house you under his own roof. Bachelor, you know."

Linnea closed her eyes and prayed for patience.

"I know," Linnea said. "You have not explained why you are here, Father. Or where you are staying."

"Silly chit," he said fondly. "I am staying here with you, of course. Lady Augusta was your mother's dearest friend for all that she has always detested me, and she can show me a little hospitality. Now, tell me how much you have missed your papa."

"No!"

He looked crestfallen.

"You have not missed me?" he asked plaintively.

"Of course, I have missed you. But you cannot stay with me. You and Lady Augusta cannot be together for two minutes without quarreling, and Lord Stoke made it very plain—"

"Lord Stoke is a pompous ass!" Lord Wrenthorpe declared to all who cared to listen. A twittering broke out all around them and Linnea wished the floor would open and swallow her up. "The sprig is not worthy to carry my old friend Stoke's boots!"

"On that," Lord Stoke said amiably as he materialized at Linnea's side, "we may agree."

"Ah, *there* you are, my boy," Lord Wrenthorpe said genially. He was foxed enough that he was unaware that Lord Stoke might have reason to be insulted. "I was just telling my girl here—"

But what he was just telling his girl was destined to remain a mystery for the time being, for Linnea's father hiccuped once and his portly frame began to buckle.

"Papa!" cried Linnea, grabbing at his arm.

Lord Stoke caught him by his armpits and managed to hold him upright. Lord Wrenthorpe's head fell back, and he began snoring on Lord Stoke's shoulder.

"Oh, Papa," Linnea said with a sigh of affectionate despair as she touched her father's face.

"Call my carriage," Lord Stoke said to one of the footmen who had come to lend his assistance.

By that time, Lord Wrenthorpe revived a little.

"Linnea," he said.

"I am here, Papa."

"Come along, now, Lord Wrenthorpe," Lord Stoke said in a commanding voice. "We will just take you out to the carriage now, and my men will see you to your lodging."

"I have no lodging," Lord Wrenthorpe said with great dignity.

Lord Stoke shared a long look with Linnea.

"Tell my coachman to take him to my house," he said to the footmen. He turned to Linnea. "For the time being," he added for her benefit.

She bowed her head in acknowledgment.

"I will go with him," she said, starting to follow.

Lord Stoke caught her hand.

"He does not need you," he said softly. "My men will see him to bed, and he is likely to sleep until morning. There is no reason for you to miss the ball. Otherwise, I have wasted my precious time bringing you into fashion."

"We cannot have that," she said dryly.

Six

Everard frowned when he saw his aunt and Lady Linnea in conversation with an elderly peer. It was plain from Aunt Augusta's animation that she was doing her best to encourage the couple to dance, and Linnea smiled at the old court card as if he were the answer to a maiden's prayers.

At that moment, pretty little Elvira Warren, his aunt's neighbor, flounced up to Everard and asked if he would attend the Venetian breakfast her mother was giving the following day. He vaguely recalled receiving an invitation and resigned himself to making an appearance for politeness's sake since the girl made a point of asking him about it.

Lord, he thought as he smiled mechanically at Miss Warren and watched his aunt and Lady Linnea from the corner of his eye, surely Aunt Augusta would not try to promote *that* match. Old Ormsley was sixty if he was a day! Everard's repugnance increased when he saw, after Ormsley's laughing departure, that Linnea was introduced to another man in his vigorous fifties who had children so diabolical they were rumored to have driven no less than two stepmothers and three governesses into residence at Bedlam.

That did it.

Everard crossed the room to Linnea's side, much to the dismay of the ravishing Miss Warren, who believed until that moment that he was hanging on her every word.

"Charming party, Aunt," Everard said to Lady Augusta,

who regarded him with astonishment. "Your servant, Fleetwood. Lady Linnea, this is our dance, I believe."

Linnea was surprised, but she put her hand on his arm and allowed him to take her away.

"My aunt said she was inviting a score of suitable bachelors to this ball for your inspection," he said when the dance had begun. "Were they all out of town? This last one is toothless *and* bald, and older than Methuselah. Why has my aunt not contrived to introduce you to any bachelor younger than your own father?"

"I'll have you know," she said demurely, "that Lord Ormsley thinks my eyes quite stunning. They remind him of sapphires twinkling in the sunlight."

"So? I said he was *bald*, not *blind*."

"He is not so bad as all that."

"He is, and you know it," he said uncompromisingly.

She narrowed her eyes at him.

"Well, you are proving rather hard to please, my lord. I was under the distinct impression you were eager to see me marry any one of them, for the sooner I do, the sooner I am off your hands."

"A good point," he said, "especially since *my* head will be in the nuptial noose if you fail to attract one of them."

She gave him a look of exasperation.

"You know very well I do not mean to hold you to *that*," she said archly. "I intend to rule the roost, of course, and a more mature gentleman should prove much more tractable than a younger one."

"Indeed? I did not notice that your father is especially tractable."

"Touché," she said with a reluctant smile.

"Speaking of Lord Wrenthorpe, I am fairly certain I made it plain to both of you that he was to stay out of trouble in Leicestershire."

Linnea stiffened.

"He is *my* father not yours. He is not obliged to obey you. I will say, though, it was kind of you to have him conveyed to your house, although I suppose you will throw him out in the street tomorrow."

"No. But I shall do so if I find him in residence at my house for longer than two weeks."

"Two weeks!"

"Do not be alarmed. I shall permit him to come back for your wedding, of course. I am not a complete ogre."

"You are *too* kind, Lord Stoke," Linnea said, looking daggers at him.

"My good girl," he said with raised eyebrows. "How am I to bring you into fashion if you will persist in looking so Friday-faced in my company?"

She had to smile at that.

"That is better," Everard said approvingly. "Do not tell me you would rather be dancing with one of those elderly relics my aunt is so assiduously trying to force upon you. You may call me a coxcomb if you please, but that would be doing it *much* too brown."

"No, indeed. But my time would be better spent dancing with Lord Ormsley. I am not in my first youth, as everyone never tires of telling me, which makes the task of finding a husband the more difficult. I am the perfect age, as I am certain either Lady Augusta or Mrs. Montclair can tell you, for a second or even third wife, but rather too long in tooth to expect to be a younger man's first."

"What nonsense," he scoffed.

"Well, I do like to think I have a *few* good years left," she said, smiling up at him.

He relinquished her to another partner after the dance, only to fall alive into the clutches of Elvira Warren and her ambitious mother once again.

Everard attended to Miss Warren's chatter with half an ear and shared his favors impartially between her and several other young ladies before going off with her to another country dance. He could hardly avoid doing so without giving offense.

His eyes kept returning to Linnea.

He could not ask her to dance again because no unmarried young woman could stand up with any gentleman for more than two dances without inviting gossip, but when it was time to go into supper he managed to carry her off right out from old Ormsley's nose.

"What have I done to annoy Aunt Augusta?" he asked Linnea.

"You know she has great hopes of Lord Ormsley for me, and she had already arranged for me to go into supper with him. *You* were intended for Miss Warren."

"Why?" he asked, genuinely puzzled.

"Because Lady Augusta says she is the twin of . . . a physical type to which you are attracted."

It took him a moment to understand, and he gave Lady Linnea credit for being reluctant to say the name of his lost love aloud in case he found it too painful.

Miss Warren was petite, blond, and demure in appearance. She had a sweet face and in many eyes, he supposed, she bore a strong resemblance to his dear Elizabeth, who had died at the tender age of eighteen, about Miss Warren's own age. He had not noticed the resemblance before, he surmised, for two reasons.

One, he had resisted so many attempts to lure him into the parson's mousetrap that most of the females of his acquaintance, by and large, had given him up as a lost cause, and this had lured him into a false sense of security with respect to such stratagems.

Two, Miss Warren may *look* like Elizabeth, but her superficial conversation and irritating, artificial titter could not have made her more unlike the woman he had once expected to marry.

"Miss Warren," Linnea added, "was *born* to be a countess, according to Lady Augusta. She is determined to help her make a grand match."

Not with me, Everard thought with a mental shudder.

"Aunt Augusta is a good deal too busy," he said with

some asperity. "If I take a notion to marry, I will choose my own bride, thank you very much!"

"Now you know how it feels to be in my shoes," Linnea said smugly. "Unfortunately, we beggars who are past our prime cannot afford to be choosers."

Everard flinched. Linnea apparently considered herself quite firmly on the shelf at five-and-twenty. She must view him at six-and-thirty as positively ancient. Rather a member of Lord Ormsley's generation, he feared.

Since their arrival in the supper room put an end to their private conversation, they began talking about books and architecture, interests they had in common, and the meal passed most agreeably.

Lord Stoke was an entertaining conversationalist, and Linnea was so animated that Lady Augusta, noticing this with disapproval, determined to give Linnea a hint as soon as the company returned to the ballroom.

"I should like a word with you, Linnea," she said, interrupting Linnea's conversation with another young lady.

"Of course, Lady Augusta," Linnea said, puzzled. She . excused herself from her companion and followed her godmother from the room.

"My dear child," she said as soon as they were alone, "I hope you will not take it amiss if I give you a hint for your own good."

"A hint?"

"About my nephew. I hope you are not refining too much upon the flattering attention he has shown you tonight. I would not want you to think that Everard—in short, he has such universally pleasing manners that many a young lady has mistaken mere civility for something deeper."

"So Mrs. Montclair has already warned me," Linnea said. Obviously Linnea's behavior had been rather less circumspect with respect to Lord Stoke than she had thought. The last thing she wanted was to give the appearance that she was setting her cap for her former fiancé's brother.

How foolish she would look! "I am persuaded Lord Stoke was merely trying to oblige *you* by being kind to me. You did say he has so much influence with the *ton* that one dance with him could bring me into fashion."

Lady Augusta looked mollified.

"Well, I *am* obliged to him. But now that he has danced with you twice, he has done his duty and so I shall tell him."

Linnea was powerless to stop Lady Augusta from speaking her mind to her own nephew, and it was with a sinking heart that she watched that formidable matron single him out.

"Everard, I know you are only trying to help, but you are doing the girl more ill than good, I fear," Lady Augusta told him after she made sure no one was listening to their conversation.

"What *are* you talking about?" he asked guardedly.

"Linnea. You have been sitting in her pocket all evening. I shall be very cross if you make her fall in love with you."

"Rubbish," he said, annoyed.

"She has been hurt badly enough. She has a fool for a father. Your brother jilted her. Her dowry is gone, and her prospects are virtually nonexistent. It was a kind gesture to bring her to London so she could find another husband. It was *exceedingly* kind of you to dance with her tonight. But you must not make her dissatisfied with the class of suitor someone in her situation is likely to attract. Escorting her into supper, although I have no doubt it was kindly meant, was unwise. I have not seen her so animated since she first became engaged to your brother."

"I have not danced with Lady Linnea to oblige *you,* Aunt, or because I feel guilty about my brother jilting her, or for any other reason except that I enjoy her company," Everard said, irritated.

"Everard!" Lady Augusta exclaimed. "You will never tell me that you have conceived a *tendre* for Lady Linnea! That father alone would *ruin* you within a year of your marriage!"

Everard held his temper in check with great difficulty.

"I did *not* say I wished to marry her. I simply said I enjoy her company. But to please you, I will not speak another word to her for the rest of the evening."

"Good," said Lady Augusta. "And I will thank you to stop looking daggers at me."

"I beg your pardon," he said, smiling for the benefit of the rest of the guests and leaving his aunt's side to spend the rest of the interminable evening flirting elegantly with all the prettiest ladies. Except one.

Linnea caught him looking at her once and smiled involuntarily. He retaliated with a smile of such singular sweetness that she resolved *nothing* must deter her from her intention of avoiding his company for the duration of the evening.

It was her purpose in London to find a man she could tolerate and marry him without delay, to their mutual benefit.

Infatuation was the deceptive emotion that had led her to believe Michael would remain faithful to her unto death. She would be an utter fool to trust her feelings for Lord Stoke.

Linnea, to her surprise, found that Lord Stoke's efforts to bring her into fashion appeared to have worked. After supper, she was invited by several personable gentlemen to dance. In between sets, she chatted with the matrons about their houses, their gardens, their children, and their tiresome husbands.

Everard noted with approval that while the other young ladies tossed their curls and laughed vivaciously, all the while looking around the room to see who was watching them, Lady Linnea never practiced these arts.

Her expression was thoughtful as she drew out her companions, and when they talked to her, her eyes never left their faces.

Everard began to perceive that Michael was an even greater fool than he had previously thought.

As he nodded politely to the overdressed debutante who

was simpering at him at the moment, he wished he had not promised his aunt he would stay away from Lady Linnea for the rest of the evening.

He observed that the gentlemen who asked her to dance after supper were far younger than the old court cards his aunt had been throwing at her. He told himself he should be pleased, to no avail. How ironic if his attentions to her truly *had* brought her into fashion.

And Linnea, seeing Lord Stoke's companion bat him playfully on the arm with her fan and look up at him adoringly, began to perceive that his aunt was right.

Lord Stoke was entirely too kind to repulse the attentions of any susceptible lady.

Linnea was determined not to embarrass him or, indeed, herself, by falling in love with him.

Seven

The next day, a stone-faced Lady Augusta observed from the upper stairway of her town house as Lord Wrenthorpe handed his hat to a footman and started to surrender a visiting card to her butler.

"Lord Wrenthorpe," she said glacially.

The earl looked up at her with a comical grimace of dismay. He was still, despite the passage of fifty-odd years, a handsome man in a craggy sort of way.

Too bad he was a scandalous old reprobate, and Augusta despised him.

"Good morning, Lady Augusta," Lord Wrenthorpe said, politely enough. "I have come to see my daughter."

Augusta was well aware he hoped to sneak into the house, see Linnea, and sneak back out again without being subjected to the piece of Augusta's mind she so dearly longed to give him. She restrained herself, for the present, from telling him what she thought of his waistcoat, which was more suited to a stripling of twenty than a gentleman of mature years and figure.

"Of course," Lady Augusta said as she descended the staircase. At the bottom she said to the footman, "Desire Lady Linnea to come into the parlor. Her father has come to pay her a visit."

When the footman was gone, Lady Augusta ushered the earl into the parlor, seated herself on the sofa, and indicated an armchair opposite.

"What possessed you to come to London?" she demanded. "You must know you are not welcome here."

"Lady Augusta," he said with a self-effacing grin as he lowered himself into the armchair, "hospitable as always."

"Well, I do not like you, Lord Wrenthorpe. I never have, and I never will. You are responsible for my dearest friend's death, and if I had my way, I would see you hanged for it."

The mischief fled from Lord Wrenthorpe's eyes and left them bleak.

"My wife died in childbirth as you well know. Christ, Augusta. You've always had an adder's tongue."

"She would not have died if you had not worn her out with one unsuccessful pregnancy after another in your single-minded selfishness. You were so determined to have a son, and her death is what came of it. I hope you are happy now that you are all alone in the world."

"I am not alone. I have Linnea," he said stonily.

"And look how well you have taken care of her," Lady Augusta scoffed. "Not only have you failed to secure the succession, but you have gambled away the unentailed property and your fortune as well so that she is forced to find a husband or starve!"

He stood.

"I do not have to take this venom from you," he snapped.

"Where did you spend the night? In the gutter?" she jibed.

"At Lord Stoke's house," Wrenthorpe said. "He was good enough to offer me his hospitality for two weeks, at which time he will throw me into the street if I am not gone by then."

He gave her a grin.

"No matter. Two weeks will be ample time for my purposes."

He turned to the doorway to see Linnea enter the room. She was slightly breathless, as if she had been running.

Linnea knew better than to leave her father and her godmother together in the same room for fear that bloody murder would come of it.

"Do not look so worried, darling," Lord Wrenthorpe said, standing to enfold his daughter in his arms. He kissed her on the cheek. "Pretty gown. I approve."

"Thank you, Papa," she said, seating herself on the sofa next to her godmother and smoothing her yellow muslin skirts.

"Eh, you are a stunner, girl. Just like your mother," he said sentimentally.

"Thank you again," she said. "Now, Papa, tell me why you have come to London against Lord Stoke's express wishes. Did you miss me that much?"

"Can you doubt it, my love? But, in truth, I came to mend our fortunes. I do not know why I did not think of this scheme before."

"Mend our fortunes," Linnea repeated faintly. "No, Papa. You promised me! No more gaming!"

"When have you known me to break my word?" he demanded as he drew himself up to his full height. Lady Augusta gave a vulgar snort, and Linnea looked rueful.

Lord Wrenthorpe seemed to deflate a little.

"Ah, well," he said with a sigh. "But I am about to make it up to you, girl. After Lord Stoke took you away, I realized we are going about the business all wrong. You do not need a husband."

Lady Augusta's brows drew together.

"You are still intoxicated!" she declared. "*Every* girl needs a husband!"

Lord Wrenthorpe regarded her with disdain.

"As I was saying before I was interrupted, Linnea," he said, "you do not need a husband. *I* need a wife!"

"You doddering old fool." Lady Augusta sniffed. "You are senile!"

"Think about it, Linnea," he said, ignoring Lady Augusta. "Why should you be dependent upon Stoke's charity—I know it galls you as much as it galls me—and feel obliged to marry some fellow who doesn't half deserve you simply because you are getting on in years and need a husband to take care of you?"

"Do not spare my feelings, by all means," she said humorously.

"But if *I* find a rich young bride, *I* will take care of you. And I am still well able to, er, well . . . That is, I am still able to avail myself of the opportunity to father an heir and secure the succession. You can take your time finding a husband, one who will suit you. And *I* will provide you with a dowry so you do not have to accept one from Lord Stoke."

For a moment, the two ladies stared at him in awe.

Lady Augusta found her voice first.

"That is the most outlandish thing I have ever heard," she screeched. "A rich young bride, indeed! And where are you going to find this accommodating young woman, may I ask?"

The earl made a sweeping gesture with one hand.

"The easiest thing in the world is to find a bride during the Season. Every heiress in the country is in London looking for a husband." He grinned. "Well, here I am!"

Linnea gave him a fond smile and rose to kiss him on the cheek.

That explained the fancy waistcoat, the high shirt points, the obscenely tight pantaloons.

"That is very sweet and thoughtful of you, Papa," she said kindly. "I know you regret losing your fortune, but I don't want *you* to have to get married in a hurry just to take care of me, either."

At that moment, Lady Augusta's butler appeared in the doorway and, at Lady Augusta's nod of assent, handed his mistress a visiting card.

"The gentleman asks if you are receiving, my lady," he told her.

Lady Augusta emerged from her perusal of the card, wreathed in smiles.

"How absolutely delightful! Linnea, darling. Guess who has come to pay his respects."

"I could not possibly," Linnea said.

Lord Ormsley entered the room with a dainty bouquet of pink and yellow hothouse roses in his hand.

"Silly ass," hissed Lord Wrenthorpe to Linnea. His brows lowered alarmingly. "I hope he is here to court Lady Augusta and not you."

"Papa," said Linnea in a shocked undervoice.

"Lady Augusta," Lord Ormsley said, bowing in the older lady's direction as he carried the bouquet to Linnea. "And, Lady Linnea," he added. "These are for you."

"Lovely!" Linnea said, bending to sniff them. "How generous of you, my lord."

"A pleasure, my dear," he said as he surrendered the bouquet to a maid. "Would you care to go driving in the park?"

"What a charming idea," said Lady Augusta.

"Yes, I would like that very—" Linnea began at the same time until her words were cut off by an exclamation of annoyance from her father.

"Here, now, Ormsley," Lord Wrenthorpe scoffed. "You should be ashamed of yourself. You are older than I am. You've buried three wives already. Have you no decency, man, to be courting a girl less than half of your age?"

Lord Ormsley's mouth opened and closed, giving Linnea a view of pink gums interspersed with several lonely looking teeth.

"Besides, the girl hasn't a dowry," Lord Wrenthorpe said triumphantly. "I gambled it all away, so you are wasting your time."

"Papa," cried Linnea. She gave her father a look of reproof. "Papa's sense of humor is somewhat . . . unusual," she added to Lord Ormsley. "If you will be kind enough to wait, I will just go and fetch my bonnet. I shall be gone only a moment, I promise you."

The gentleman bowed and turned affronted eyes to

Linnea's father, but did not lower himself to bandying words with him.

"Lord Ormsley, do be seated," Lady Augusta said. "Lord Wrenthorpe," she added with a glare at Linnea's father, "was just leaving." When Lord Wrenthorpe merely looked mulish, she snapped, "At once!"

Lord Wrenthorpe huffed out of the room.

"Damned fellow has barely a tooth left in his head," he grumbled rather too audibly as he went.

"Linnea's father has always been overprotective," Lady Augusta said in an effort to smooth Lord Ormsley's ruffled feathers. "Fortunately, dear Linnea more closely resembles her excellent mother."

"Something for which to be thankful," Lord Ormsley replied tartly. He rose when Linnea came into the room with a charming confection of blond straw and green tulle on her dark curls.

"What a lovely day for a drive," she said to Lord Ormsley. "It is so kind of you to invite me."

He opened the door for her and she sailed out, addressing some remark to him over her shoulder. She gasped when she walked right into a hard chest and raised her eyes to Lord Stoke's as he caught her elbows to keep her from falling down.

Caught between their bodies was a sad crush of white lilies. The sweet, exotic fragrance rose between them. Golden pollen stained the earl's dark coat.

"Oh, Lord Stoke!" she cried. "I am so sorry. I was not looking where I was going."

"No harm done," he said, "except to the flowers."

"How beautiful they are," she said, gathering the blossoms in her gloved hands. "And what a lovely fragrance."

Lord Ormsley scowled at the younger man. The bouquet of lilies was much larger than the one he had brought.

"I will just have one of the maids float them in a glass bowl, your lordship," said the butler, who had watched the disaster unfold from the doorway, as he relieved them of the crushed flowers.

A few moments later, Everard sipped tea as he watched his aunt pace the floor in front of him.

"Do sit down, I beg of you, Aunt Augusta. You are starting to make me bilious," he told her.

"Whatever possessed you to tell Linnea's father he could stay in your house?" she demanded. "Why did you not pack him off to Leicestershire at once?"

"Because he is a grown man, and I have no right to do anything of the kind."

"Do you know what scheme the old rogue has afoot now?" she asked. "He is to marry an heiress, if you please, father a son to secure the succession, and provide a dowry for Linnea himself so she need not marry in haste. Did you ever hear anything so preposterous? Then he no doubt will gamble the heiress's fortune away, for good measure, if he can find anyone so foolish as to marry him."

"I wish him well," Everard said with lifted eyebrows. "Meanwhile, it will do no harm to let him stay with me for two weeks. He was my father's closest friend, you will recall."

"You are too good," she said, "which practically invites all sorts of indigent connections to hang upon your sleeve."

"I only do my duty," he said with a shrug, forbearing to mention that she cost him as much as any of them. "The ball went very well. I congratulate you. And Lady Linnea seemed to show to great advantage from the number of bouquets in this room."

Indeed, there were four, not counting the large crystal bowl of floating lily blossoms a smiling maid brought into the room to place on a low table.

Lady Augusta regarded the bowl with a surprised look. "Now, that is an unusual arrangement. Quite pretty."

She rose and sniffed the air above the bowl with satisfaction.

"Is there a card?" she asked the maid, who had bobbed a curtsy and was about to leave the room. "I do not see one."

"No. I brought them," Everard admitted.

Augusta raised one disapproving brow.

"The lilies are for both of you," he explained, "to congratulate you upon the success of the ball."

A bald-faced lie. He had thought only of Linnea when he purchased them.

"I see. How very thoughtful, Everard," Aunt Augusta said, relaxing into a smile.

Eight

The sight of Lieutenant Michael Montclair in his dress uniform with his chestnut hair glimmering under the light of six crystal chandeliers and his hazel eyes sparkling with pleasure as he bent to whisper something in his bride's ear made Linnea's heart clutch in her breast for a moment even as she forced a smile to her lips for the benefit of the gossips she could see watching her avidly for her reaction.

She *refused* to wear her heart on her sleeve for this man.

Mrs. Montclair, the happy bridegroom's cousin, Phoebe, had described the Spanish bride as being in Linnea's own style, and Linnea supposed she should be flattered.

Certainly, the radiant bride was beautiful in an elaborate crimson ball gown trimmed in the Spanish style with black lace. Instead of choosing to blend in with all the young English misses dressed in slim gowns in light spring colors, Vittoria Montclair celebrated her foreign birth and her status as a married lady by wearing clothing far too flashy to be appropriate for a debutante.

"What a magnificent gown," Linnea observed dutifully to Lady Augusta.

"That's my brave girl," that lady said approvingly under her breath. She gave Linnea's hand a squeeze of reassurance.

Linnea was relieved. She had not known *how* she would react upon seeing her former fiancé. It would not have done at all for her to burst into tears. For that reason, she and Lady Augusta had deliberately timed their arrival late, so they would not reach Lord Stoke's mansion until well after the receiving line had been disbanded.

"The worst is over now," Lady Augusta said comfortingly. She gave Linnea a coy look. "At *this* ball, I promise you, you shall not lack for partners."

"May I have this dance, Lady Linnea?" a personable gentlemen, who had been introduced to her upon her arrival as one of Lord Stoke's friends, asked with a polite bow.

Linnea's lips quirked.

How like Lord Stoke to solicit a succession of gentlemen to ensure that Linnea would not be a wallflower at her former fiancé's ball. Linnea accepted this kindness with just as much enjoyment as she did the elegant new gown of periwinkle blue she deliberately had saved for first wearing on this occasion.

"I would be delighted, Mr. Whitcomb," she told the blond, blue-eyed man as she accepted the arm he extended to her.

He was an elegant dancer and an excellent conversationalist. When he was supplanted by a dark-haired cavalry officer whom Aunt Augusta later told her was a fellow officer of Lord Stoke's when he had served with a smart regiment, Mr. Whitcomb did her the honor of asking her in advance for another dance later on.

"Where have you been all my life?" the handsome cavalry officer asked Linnea unoriginally when they had been dancing for several moments.

She merely smiled, for he had to know very well that she had spent the past few years in Leicestershire, hiding out with her father from the tradesmen. Everyone else certainly did.

At one point when she was going down to the dance floor with Mr. Whitcomb, who had claimed a waltz as his second dance, she came face-to-face with Michael and his bride. His ruddy complexion went stark white at the sight of her.

Linnea felt heat rise to her face.

Since no one else apparently was going to, Linnea ended the frozen tableau by saying tartly to her erstwhile betrothed, "Let us not make a piece of work of this, Michael. Move aside, if you please."

At that, her partner was recalled to his responsibilities and gently touched Michael on the shoulder as a signal for him to move. Then he escorted Linnea to the dance floor.

It gave Linnea infinite satisfaction to hear Michael say, "She did not look so well when *I* was betrothed to her."

She wondered how his bride reacted to *that*.

From across the room, Everard watched Linnea smile into the eyes of his friend with admiration.

The girl had acquitted herself well at her first meeting with Michael after the severing of their betrothal. And she certainly gave every appearance of having a good time in the company of his friends, whom he had enlisted to dance with her. Tonight, at least, she would not waste her time with a collection of old court cards.

Oddly, this observation did not give him much satisfaction.

He had no time to dwell on the reason for this because a shrill scream rose above the music and conversation in the ballroom. He turned at once and ran for the doorway to the gardens, where a small crowd had gathered.

Everard gave a long-suffering sigh, for Lord Wrenthorpe, much worse for drink, had Elvira Warren cornered against a tree and was placing ardent kisses all over her horrified face.

"Come along, Lord Wrenthorpe," Everard said as he took the man's arm in a firm grip. He intended to escort the gentleman unobtrusively into the house, where he could hand him over to a footman who would see him to bed, but Miss Warren thwarted him by throwing herself into Everard's unwilling arms and weeping hysterically all over his chest.

"He *attacked* me," she sobbed.

"I did *not*," Lord Wrenthorpe said, sounding embarrassed and a little hurt. "She encouraged my advances. Told me she needed some fresh air."

"To get *away* from you," she shouted. She balled one fist and raised her arm as if she might strike him.

Remembering in time that she was a frail feminine flower, she dropped her arm, turned back to Everard, and cried, "It was so terrible!" as she threw herself on his chest again.

"There, there, love," said the girl's mother after she had forced her way through the crowd of gapers. Everard hoped she would take her daughter away, but she merely patted her on the back. The ambitious Mrs. Warren had devoted the best part of two weeks trying to get Elvira into his arms, Everard knew, and she was not about to remove her from them now that she had achieved her goal.

To Everard's relief, Linnea walked out into the garden with her partner in tow, pried Miss Warren from her death grip on Everard, and gave her a gentle push toward her mother.

"Lord Stoke, perhaps you will instruct a footman to escort Mrs. Warren and her daughter to a bedchamber where Miss Warren can regain her composure in privacy before she rejoins the party," Linnea suggested.

She turned to her father.

"Come along, Papa," she said kindly. "You have not danced with me yet. I have worn poor Mr. Whitcomb out with the waltz, and he will be glad to relinquish me to you."

"Very true, sir," that gentleman said, rising to the occasion as he placed a companionable arm across Lord Wrenthorpe's shoulders to flank the elder man's other side.

The trio started to move toward the door. "Your daughter was just telling me . . ."

Linnea looked back at Everard.

"Miss Warren," she reminded him.

Since the girl looked ready to throw herself on his chest again, he moved with some haste to signal a footman to escort mother and daughter to a bedchamber.

"I saw her," Everard said to Linnea later. "She encouraged him."

Linnea looked up from the glass of lemonade her father had procured for her after their dance before he went off to solicit a new partner.

"Miss Warren," Everard explained at her look of inquiry. "She was having a jolly time waltzing with him until they went out into the gardens. I can see why he was misled. At the risk of sounding like a conceited coxcomb again, I believe she was trying, at her mother's instigation, to make me jealous."

"Thank you for telling me that," she said with a sigh. "Poor Papa. All the mothers are guarding their daughters from him."

"I heard that he is looking for an heiress."

Linnea sighed again.

"Along with every other man in England."

"My friend Whitcomb seems quite taken with you."

"Well, I am quite taken with him," she said, brightening. "He was very good with Papa just now."

"He is heir to a comfortable fortune from his aunt, and he is on the lookout for a wife."

"A widower, is he not?"

"Yes. His wife died two years ago." Everard did not mention that the union was childless and very unhappy. Whitcomb's late wife had been a spoiled, demanding shrew. Linnea would be a vast improvement over her. "They married very young. He has told me he is looking for a sensible woman who will not cut up stiff over every little thing."

Linnea lifted her eyebrows.

"Enjoying a spot of matchmaking, are we?" she asked with an arch smile.

"Why not?" he said with a shrug. "He's a good man, and much your own age. You could do much worse."

"Yes. *Much* worse."

"Do not worry," he said. "You were promised a June wedding, and one way or another we will get you one." He looked up at someone standing behind Linnea's left shoulder. "There you are, Michael. Come to dance with Lady Linnea, are you? It is about time."

Wide-eyed, Linnea, spun around to face her faithless ex-fiancé. He bowed and extended his hand.

"Oh, I hardly think so, Lieutenant Montclair," she said, drawing back.

"Everyone is watching," Everard said between his stiffly smiling lips.

"Oh, bother!" she said with ill grace. She smiled fiercely up into Michael's eyes as she took his hand for the country dance. He flinched a little.

"You look well," he said after they had been dancing in silence for several minutes.

"Thank you," she said. "I could say the same. Marriage obviously agrees with you."

"Linnea," he said reproachfully.

"Merely an observation."

"It was not my intention to hurt you. I am more sorry than I can express," he said as the movement of the dance brought them together again.

"You certainly are," she said coldly, but still smiling. "Whatever possessed you to ask me to dance?"

"Who, actually."

"Lord Stoke," she said with a sigh. "Your brother is the *busiest* man of my acquaintance. I suppose he thought it would quell the gossips if we were seen dancing together."

"That, too. But mostly he thought you deserved a

chance to tell me what a blackguard I am for breaking our engagement."

"That is just the problem," she said. "You never did break our engagement, did you? You simply married someone else and left it to your brother to tell me."

"I meant to write. I was fighting a war, you know!" He had the gall to sound testy, as if *he* were the injured party.

"How long had you been married before your return?"

"Four months," he said in a small voice. "Vittoria was so brave. She followed the drum as if she had done so all her life."

"While I remained in England, waiting for you. As if I had done so all my life," Linnea said mockingly. "Please spare me your raptures of praise for your wife. The strains of civility will extend only so far without breaking."

"You do look very well," he said lamely. "I like this new style of hairdressing. And your gown is very pretty. I should not be surprised if Whitcomb offers for you. He seemed quite attentive. Then we may all be comfortable. Everard is quite set on the match."

"Is he, indeed? Why?"

"Because he has taken a notion that he must marry you himself if you cannot find a husband by June 19, and we all know Everard is a confirmed bachelor. Did you really insist that he do so?"

"I was angry," she said. "I wanted to punish someone, and you were not close at hand."

"Everard was quite devoted to Elizabeth once he had formed an attachment to her, so I am not surprised that he has found it difficult to entertain the prospect of marriage with another woman."

"In that, I perceive, the two of you are vastly different," she said waspishly.

"Linnea," he said again, looking ashamed.

To their mutual relief, the dance came to an end. Linnea left his arms with a smile that was not entirely forced, for there was always satisfaction in getting the last word.

Lord Stoke strode forward to intercept her before she could return to her godmother.

"Our dance, I believe," he said.

Linnea took his arm without hesitation. She had a thing or two to say to him.

"Well done, Lady Linnea," he said in congratulatory tones.

"You cannot imagine how gratified I am by your approval," she replied.

He raised his eyebrows.

"Do not be such a little prig. Next you will tell me that you derived no satisfaction whatsoever from giving my graceless brother a piece of your mind and sending him back to his wife with his tail between his legs."

She gave an involuntary huff of laughter.

"I suppose I should thank you for that," she admitted.

"Yes, you should," he said smugly. "And your dance with Michael certainly got the guests' minds off the scene between your father and Miss Warren. See, she and her mother have returned to the ballroom, and the little chit is already surrounded by admirers. With very little effort, I am certain she has persuaded herself that she is the heroine of the day."

Linnea could not help smiling.

"Is there anyone who does not dance to the tune of your piping?"

"No," he said, sounding distracted as he watched his aunt move to intercept Mrs. Warren. "I wonder what has happened to put Aunt Augusta into the hips."

Linnea raised her hand to his cheek and turned his face back to hers.

Startled, he looked down into her eyes, and she felt heat rise to her cheeks. This was an extremely intimate gesture, one that was hardly appropriate to the middle of the dance floor.

She was aware suddenly, of the texture of his skin

under her gloved fingers, the fragrance of his cologne, the sudden flash of heat in his eyes.

"Lady Augusta is a grown woman and can take care of herself for the space of a dance without having you rush over to mediate whatever quarrel she has with Mrs. Warren."

He relaxed, and she drew her hand away.

"I must seem very high-handed and overbearing to you," he said ruefully.

"High-handed and overbearing? You?" she said mockingly. "How could I possibly think such a thing?"

When the dance came to an end, he took her arm and walked her out to the gardens.

"What are you doing?" she asked when they were out in the cool night. The gardens were illuminated with colorful little lanterns shining along the paths of gorgeously blooming roses.

"Taking your advice and avoiding Aunt Augusta. Do you mind?"

"No, of course not. It is a refreshing change not to be stared at by your hopeful guests looking for a sign of hysteria or collapse over your brother's betrayal." She gave a snort of contempt. "Did you see the way she *looks* at him? Like a puppy wagging her tail before her master, as if he were the sun, moon, and stars all at once. Have you ever seen anything like it?"

"Vittoria?" he guessed. "Yes. You used to look at him exactly the same way."

"Oh, come now!" she objected. "I *never*—"

"Exactly the same way." She could see the flash of his teeth in the lantern light. "And I assure you, you looked just as silly."

"I was very young," she said ruefully. "That must be my excuse."

"Then you are not still in love with him?"

"No," she said. "I question sometimes whether I ever was in love with him. It was just so *perfect*. My first ball.

The handsome cavalry officer to sweep me off my feet. Our fathers' approval. The parties. I have come to the conclusion that I'm a terribly shallow person. My heart is hardly broken, I assure you."

Especially not when she was with Lord Stoke, who had taken her hand and was making her pulse flutter under his warm fingers in the fragrant garden.

"I am glad to hear that," he said, and kissed her.

Linnea gasped against his lips and drew back. She covered her mouth with both of her hands.

"I apologize," he said, sounding mortified.

"No," she said. "I was surprised, that is all."

"Of course," he said woodenly. "Shall we go back?"

He kissed her. Lord Stoke *kissed* her. Linnea could not believe it. *Why* had she drawn back like a little ninny instead of savoring it? But his lips had been so warm, and her heart had given a gigantic leap as if it would stop altogether.

She knew now that she had never, not even for a moment, been in love with Michael, for none of his kisses had affected her like this.

"Lord Stoke—" she began.

He raised a hand to silence her.

"You must forgive me," he said with a brittle smile. "I am as susceptible as any other man when faced with a pretty girl in the moonlight. I meant no insult."

"Lord Stoke—"

"Let us go inside," he said, offering his arm.

Linnea did not want to go inside. She wanted to stay out in the gardens and stroll among the roses with Lord Stoke in the hope that he would kiss her again.

But he wasn't going to.

He was *sorry* he had kissed her, and no wonder. She had behaved as if she had never been kissed in her life, which was almost true because Michael no longer counted. She wasn't in love with Michael. She was in love with—

She was in love with bossy, interfering, maddening Lord

Stoke, and she was very much afraid that she would be for the rest of her life.

Trembling, she accepted his arm, careful to keep any part of her body from brushing his as they entered the house.

Nine

Whatever *had* possessed him to kiss her?

Well, Everard knew the answer to that.

She had been so pretty. So brave. So sad beneath her bravado.

He thought, when he bent to taste her lips, it was only because he felt sorry for her and wanted to make her feel better.

Instead of making her feel better, he had forced himself to face a truth he had been pushing into the back of his mind since he had first seen her, chin up and expecting the worst, in Leicestershire.

Everard was in love with Lady Linnea.

And he absolutely repulsed her. She had actually rubbed his kiss from her lips with her gloved fingers.

Not that he was surprised. He had bullied and manipulated her from the start. And he was eleven years older than she. Everard knew there wasn't a matchmaking mother in England who wouldn't be happy to sacrifice her tender young daughter to a much older man in exchange for the cachet of a coronet and a leading role in society for her little darling, but Lady Linnea deserved a man who had something left to give. His large, demanding family exhausted him.

He looked down at the top of her head. She had not said a word to him since they came inside, and no wonder.

Only a man without honor would force himself on a

woman who was so vulnerable. And, despite her show of spirit, she *was* vulnerable.

"Lady Linnea, I have said I am sorry."

"I know you are," she said.

"You want to go home, I imagine. I will send for your carriage and find Aunt Augusta for you."

"Why should I?" she said. "The ball is in full swing, and there are bachelors running tame on the ground all around me. Tally-ho! Ah, there is Lord Ormsley." She made a *moue* of disappointment. "Oh. I forgot he was annoyed with Papa. He gave me the cut direct. How very uncivil of him."

"Lady Linnea—"

"No matter," she said brightly. "There are more. Have you no more friends you can bully into dancing with me, or have I run through them already?"

"I will see what I can do," he said, nettled.

"Never mind. Here is Lord Fleetwood."

Lord Fleetwood. Fifty if he was a day. And with children so incorrigible that they had sent three nursemaids into strong convulsions in as many months. The old rogue actually *boasted* about it at his club.

"Not him," he snapped. "Anyone but him."

"He is a very charming man," she snapped right back. "And what do you care whom I marry as long as I am off your hands?"

Everard gritted his teeth and bowed to his lordship when he came at once to claim Linnea. She smiled at him in coy invitation and went off with every appearance of pleasure to dance with him.

"Linnea is so lovely tonight," his Aunt Augusta said complacently from behind him. "Between us, we have done a marvelous job of firing her off. Young Whitcomb seems taken with her."

"He is too easygoing," Everard said sourly. "She will rule the roost, make no mistake."

"Perhaps he will not mind," Lady Augusta said. "She is a good girl, and will make him a good wife."

"She will drive him into Bedlam within a fortnight," he said.

"Nonsense! It is time he settled down. And you as well."

"I? And who have you chosen for me, now that you have disposed of Lady Linnea's future so felicitously?"

"Elvira Warren, of course! A nice biddable girl with good breeding who will be a credit for you." She patted his hand. "We were all fond of dear Elizabeth, but it is time you came out of the mopes and did your duty to your family."

"I beg your pardon, Aunt Augusta," he said, outraged that she should refer to his long, sincere mourning for his late fiancée as the mopes. "How dare you or anyone suggest that I have not done my duty to my family?"

"I suggested nothing of the kind. I merely meant to say that it is time for you to marry. You are not getting any younger."

"Do you know anyone who is?" he asked.

"You know what I mean! You do not want to end up alone."

He gave a snort of disbelief.

"With *my* family? If only I were so fortunate," he said, and rudely walked away.

"Well!" he heard her say after him in some dudgeon. "Everard, how dare you walk away from me when I am addressing you?"

He kept walking.

Linnea was dancing with Lord Fleetwood, but she gave Everard a look of defiance when she caught him watching her. He honestly could not blame her. He had done nothing but manipulate her for weeks, just as his aunt was attempting to manipulate him. *He* certainly did not like it when Aunt Augusta and his various meddling female relatives tried to inveigle him into matrimony with one simpering damsel or another.

From now on, Everard resolved, he was going to mind his own business. Lady Linnea could marry any old court card she chose since she obviously did not want his help. Or, as she had made it abundantly clear, his kisses.

His teeth clenched when he saw Whitcomb approach her again. He started forward, ready to interfere if he asked her to dance. Three dances with the same woman would declare Whitcomb's intentions before all the *ton*. Then he forced himself to relax.

The man could count, after all. Perhaps he *was* serious about Linnea.

If he was, it would be Everard's own damned fault for asking him to dance with her.

"Lord Stoke," said Mrs. Warren, interrupting his thoughts.

He glanced at Linnea and Whitcomb, who were laughing together.

"Mrs. Warren," he said, smiling at Mrs. Warren and her daughter, who had been restored to her usual beauty and cheerfulness. As host, it would do him no good to put off the inevitable, so he extended his arm to the young lady and prepared to do his duty. "I see you are quite recovered from your ordeal. May I have this dance, Miss Warren?"

She tossed her blond curls and simpered up at him.

To his annoyance, Everard saw his Aunt Augusta smile approvingly at him, as if he were a lapdog who had performed a trick particularly well at her bidding.

A few minutes in Miss Warren's company convinced Everard that if he were shackled to this girl, he would strangle her within a fortnight—if she did not poison his morning coffee first.

Fortunately, his ordeal did not last long—or, at least, this particular ordeal did not last long—for a scream erupted from the corner of the ballroom and Everard abandoned his partner to stride through the guests, who were moving in the same direction, making excited little murmurs of curiosity and consternation as they craned their necks to see what new atrocities had been committed.

At the center of the storm, not surprisingly, he found the Earl of Wrenthorpe with his arms around a laughing girl, and a stout matron demanding that he release her daughter *at once!*

"Papa!" said Linnea sternly as she stepped between her father and Everard. "Give her back!"

"But I *like* blondes," Linnea's father pouted.

"Now, if you please!"

Grudgingly he released the girl, whose arm was immediately taken in a hard grip by the matron. That woman gave the earl a look of disdain and called loudly for her carriage.

"I was only dancing with him," the girl wailed as her mother tried to drag her away. "He was so very droll! He said he is an earl, and he is not as old as the fusty old marquis you keep throwing at me."

"Everyone knows the old roué is all to pieces!" the matron said in a disastrously loud voice. "He should be ashamed of himself! And the marquis is rich and distinguished, unlike *him.*"

"Papa, perhaps you should not pursue the girls quite so enthusiastically," Linnea said, looking tired. "Why do you not escort me to the refreshment room? I am perishing for a glass of punch."

Grudgingly, he offered her his arm, and Everard gave a long sigh.

It was going to be a long two weeks with the Earl of Wrenthorpe as his houseguest.

Everard was so lost in self-pity for a moment that he was startled when a hand touched his arm.

"Harry," he said, smiling, to Mr. Whitcomb, the one who had shown such an interest in Lady Linnea. "I hope you are enjoying yourself."

"Yes, thank you," Mr. Whitcomb replied. "I do not think I have enjoyed such unusual entertainment at a ball this age. Lady Linnea is staying with Lady Augusta, is she not?"

"She is," Everard said dryly. "And I am certain that you will find her at home if you call."

"Indeed?" the other man asked eagerly. "What did she say about me?"

"She did not have to say anything. It is obvious she enjoyed dancing with you."

"I enjoyed dancing with her immensely," Mr. Whitcomb said rapturously. "Have you ever seen such eyes?"

"No. Her eyes are quite remarkable," Everard said.

"You did say she has a dowry of five thousand pounds?" Everard frowned.

"I did."

"Excellent. I shall certainly call on the young lady tomorrow," he said as he stepped jauntily away.

"I do not understand it," Lady Augusta said two days later, frowning, as she went through the post over her breakfast tea.

"What is it, Godmama?" asked Linnea as she helped herself to lovely bacon and fluffy eggs from the sideboard.

"There is no invitation for Lady Godwin's ball. I was sure we would receive it today." Her brow cleared. "Perhaps it was lost in the post."

"Perhaps," Linnea agreed, seating herself across from Lady Augusta.

"I should not be surprised if Mr. Whitcomb calls today," Lady Augusta said with a twinkle in her eye. "The bouquet of roses he sent yesterday was quite stunning. And that dashing, dark-eyed cavalry officer who attended the ball. Everard's friend. What was his name?"

"I do not remember," Linnea said. "There were a great many people at the ball."

"Yes, and trust your father to make a fool of himself before them all, chasing those young girls, the old goat! If he ruins your chances of contracting a suitable marriage, I shall never forgive him."

"You have never forgiven him, anyway," Linnea said softly.

"And I never will," Lady Augusta snapped. "When I think of what he has caused you and your poor mother to suffer—"

"He has suffered, too," Linnea said. "He loved my mother very much. And he loves me."

"That will not stop him from ruining your life," Lady Augusta said bitterly. "Everard did the right thing in taking you away from Leicestershire. I do think young Mr. Whitcomb may be the answer to all your prayers. So clever of Everard to enlist his friends to dance with you."

"Your precious Everard is a great deal too busy!" Linnea snapped. She toyed with her eggs.

"Are you not hungry?" Lady Augusta asked.

Indeed, Linnea usually heaped her breakfast plate with food and devoured it with an enthusiasm that made Lady Augusta wince.

"Not especially," Linnea said.

"My poor girl, you are not ill, are you?" Lady Augusta sounded alarmed, and Linnea smiled in spite of herself.

"No, Godmama, I am not ill," she said. "It would take more than worry about Papa or a disagreement with you to put me off my feed."

"Such an inelegant expression, my dear," Lady Augusta complained.

Linnea merely grinned and tucked into her bacon with relish.

"I still cannot understand why we have not received a card for Lady Godwin's ball," Lady Augusta said, returning to her original grievance.

She was even more perplexed that afternoon when she and her goddaughter, awaiting callers in the parlor, found the door knocker silent. And later that evening, when they attended a rout, their hostess's greeting was decidedly chilly.

Mr. Whitcomb, after disappointing the ladies that afternoon, did not call the next day or the next.

Ten

Mr. Whitcomb hung his head as Everard glared at him in disapproval over a glass of wine at their club.

"Nothing against the girl," he said, "but my aunt has threatened to disinherit me if I persist in paying my attentions to her. I can hardly risk losing her fortune for Lady Linnea's five thousand pounds."

"I thought your aunt was a recluse."

"She is. She rarely leaves her house. Unfortunately, her bosom bow is the grandmother of that silly blonde Lord Wrenthorpe had his hands all over at your ball."

"Oh."

"Oh," Mr. Whitcomb agreed sardonically.

"That's it, then," Everard said. He could hardly expect Whitcomb to offer for Linnea when to do so would mean his financial ruin.

"I do not suppose you would reconsider if I increased the dowry to ten thousand pounds," Everard said diffidently.

"Ah, so *you* are the source of the girl's dowry. I thought as much. Generous of you, but no. I hear even Lord Fleetwood has withdrawn from the lists."

Everard raised one eyebrow.

"I am glad to hear it, although I am surprised. He has been quite one of her most persistent admirers."

"He told me and a party of men in confidence over a bottle of gin that it was a pity the girl did not inherit any of her father's amorousness. Cold as a fish, he said. Apparently the fellow tried to kiss her and got frozen out for his pains."

"The randy old lecher!" Everard snapped. "I will have a word with him about bandying Lady Linnea's name all over town in such a way!"

Mr. Whitcomb jokingly cowered from the expression on his friend's face.

"Steady now, old fellow! I doubt if he's spreading it about town because it makes him look just as unappealing as it does her. And to tell you the truth, the girl shies like a nervous filly every time a man gets close to her."

"What nonsense," Everard said, although he remembered the way Linnea recoiled from his kiss all too well.

"Noticed it myself, although I attributed it to good breeding and ladylike restraint," he said. "Perhaps it is just as well my aunt won't stand for the match. No fellow wants a frigid wife in his bed, for one must have progeny, after all. Looks dashed queer if he does not. And she does not seem the type to tolerate a mistress."

"No, I think not," Everard said with a snort of reluctant amusement. He raised his glass again. This was unusually fine port.

A disturbance broke out in another room, and both men looked to the doorway to see the majordomo struggle to prevent Lord Wrenthorpe from entering.

"What do you mean, I'm not a member!" the earl blustered. "I've belonged to this club for years."

"Your membership ended two years ago, my lord," the embarrassed majordomo said, panting. "Surely you remember."

"Remember nothing of the kind," the earl said. He looked at Everard. "Stoke! Tell this fellow who I am!"

"Good evening, Lord Wrenthorpe," Everard said. He turned to the flustered majordomo. "Lord Wrenthorpe is my houseguest. Be a good man and permit him to join us for a glass of wine."

He added in a lowered voice as Lord Wrenthorpe, who took advantage of the majordomo's slackened grip to escape, advanced into the room, "One glass, and I will take him home. I promise."

"The rules, my lord—"

"No one is in this room except Mr. Whitcomb and myself. Who will know?"

"I suppose there is no harm."

"No harm at all," Everard agreed as he smoothly conveyed a folded five-pound note from his hand to the majordomo's. He then put a hand on Lord Wrenthorpe's shoulder and brought him forward to sit at the table.

"You're a good fellow," the earl said, "for all that your brother is a faithless blackguard. No offense intended."

"None taken," Everard said.

The earl squinted at Mr. Whitcomb.

"You are the fellow who has been making up to my daughter," he said. "Lady Augusta is in the deuce of a pucker because you've dropped the girl, but I do not mind. You are not good enough for her."

"I imagine no man is in a father's eyes," Mr. Whitcomb said genially. "Pretty girl, Lady Linnea. Not in my style, though, I am afraid."

The earl gave a derisive snort.

"Not rich enough for you, I take it," he said belligerently. "When I still had my fortune and my girl had a dowry of thirty thousand pounds, she would have been in your style, I have no doubt."

Mr. Whitcomb shifted uncomfortably in his chair.

"I had best take my leave," he said, standing.

"Go, then," the earl said impatiently.

"Spiritless young puppy," he added as Mr. Whitcomb scuttled away.

With true strength of character, Everard forbore to tell him that Mr. Whitcomb's reluctance to espouse Linnea had more to do with her relationship to an old man who made a spectacle of himself in society than with the deficiency of the dowry Everard had offered to settle upon her in the event of her marriage.

He poured the earl a glass of port, even though the old man already appeared the worse for drink. Everard would have him home in bed within the hour, after all.

"Thank you, lad," the earl said with a sigh. "This courting is thirsty work. What is wrong with girls nowadays? After my wife died, they were dropping into my arms like ripe plums. The only way to defend myself from them was to go to the gaming hells, where they did not allow 'em to come in."

He took a healthy drink of the port.

"Trouble is, I left it too long," he said with a sigh. "Should have married sooner. But I could not bear the thought of taking another wife for a long time after I lost Linnea's mother. Linnea takes after her, thank the Almighty. What a woman she was!"

"I am sure she was."

"Now I have no choice," the earl went on. "I have to bring myself to the sticking point because it's the only way to save Linnea from marrying a namby-pamby jackanapes such as your friend, Mr. Whitcomb."

"Perhaps if you did not try so hard," Everard suggested.

"Ha!" the earl said scornfully. "No offense, boy, but you are hardly one to be giving advice. Never married, were you?"

"No. My fiancée died while I was at war."

"I remember," the earl said, "that it was long ago. You are an earl, like me. You need an heir."

"An heir?" Everard said with a mirthless chuckle. "I have at least a half-dozen of them. There are my four brothers, and their sons into the bargain. And I would be passing my poor heir more a burden than a honey fall with my title, I assure you."

"Ah, that is why you need a good wife. The right woman can lighten any burden." The earl gave a sentimental sigh. "I had her and lost her. There will never be another woman like my Louisa."

"Here is to her," Everard said, raising his glass.

The sheen of tears glistened in the old earl's eyes.

"Bless you, boy," he said, and drank. "I cannot hope to find another like her, but I can still save my daughter from marrying someone she cannot like in desperation. There must be some girl out there who wouldn't mind marrying me to become a countess. Society has come to a pretty pass when a fellow can't sell his name and title in exchange for a decent dowry and a warm bed."

"That seems rather . . . cold-blooded," said Everard, taken aback.

"Done all the time," the earl said. "Over and over. I had hoped your brother was different, and he wanted to marry my girl for her sweet face and good heart. But he just wanted her dowry, after all."

"I think it was more than that," Everard said, "at the time."

"And I had to lose him for her," the earl said bitterly. "Well, a man makes his mistakes, but it's never too late to rectify them. Wish me luck, lad!"

On this spirited pronouncement, the earl hiccupped and his head fell forward as Everard leapt up and caught the earl's shoulders to keep his face from smashing against the tabletop.

"Come along, Wrenthorpe," Everard said softly as he hoisted the blinking earl to his feet and put a supporting arm around his shoulders. The majordomo held the door as he half led, half carried the earl out of the room.

"I understand you have increased the price on my head," Linnea told Everard the next time he came to call. He was sorry to see that the silver salver at the front door was empty of visiting cards. It apparently was true that society had decided to shun Lady Augusta and Lady Linnea.

"I had hoped the tale would not come to your ears," he said, chagrined.

"It *is* rather lowering to reflect that no gentleman can

swallow the prospect of marrying me, even for the sake of ten thousand pounds."

"I could increase it further," he said only half jokingly.

She placed her hand over his and smiled at him.

"You have been more than generous, my lord, and I thank you. I shall cancel the appointment at the church. The chance of a suitor coming forward in three weeks is extremely unlikely. Indeed, I should have canceled it before now."

At that moment, Lord Wrenthorpe burst into the parlor. For once he seemed perfectly sober.

"There you are, Stoke," he said. "I am glad to see you and Linnea together. It saves time."

"Papa?" Linnea said, frowning. "You seem upset. Is anything wrong?"

"Yes, and it is about to be set right. I have tried to no avail to find a woman of fortune willing to marry me, so Lord Stoke, as Linnea's father, I demand that you do your duty by her and marry her on June 19 in default of your brother in accordance with the spirit of the betrothal agreement signed by your father and myself."

Linnea's jaw dropped.

"Papa!"

"There is no help for it, girl. It is only fair, after all."

"Fair! How can you say so?" Linnea exclaimed.

"Marry Linnea," the earl said to Everard, "or name your friends!"

Lord Wrenthorpe looked magnificent. Sober for once, and on his paternal dignity, he had left off the fashionable garb that so ill became him and was wearing clothes suited to a gentleman of his age and rank. Apparently he had abandoned the idea of courting, thank God.

And he was right, by heaven!

"Very well, Lord Wrenthorpe. I ask you for permission to pay my addresses to your daughter."

"Lord Stoke!" Linnea cried.

"Granted!" Lord Wrenthorpe said. He shook hands with

the younger man and gave Linnea a stern look when she opened her mouth to object.

Lady Augusta came into the room.

"Have we visitors, my dear?" she said, wreathed in smiles, to Linnea. When she saw Lord Wrenthorpe, her expression relaxed into a frown. "Oh. It is only you."

Lord Wrenthorpe took her arm and guided her from the room.

"Come along, Augusta. These two young people have much to discuss."

"But—"

"I have just asked Lord Wrenthorpe for the honor of his daughter's hand in marriage," Everard said, giving his aunt a straight look. "And he has accepted me."

"Everard! Of course, I love Linnea like a daughter, but—"

"The only question," Lord Stoke said, turning to Linnea with a wry smile, "is whether the lady herself will accept me."

"Prettily done, upon my word," Linnea's father said with satisfaction as he ushered a gaping Augusta from the room. She was opening and closing her mouth like a landed fish, and Everard knew it was only a matter of time before she found her voice. Lord Wrenthorpe obviously was determined to remove her from the room before that happened.

"Lord Stoke, I assure you I do not expect you to make this sacrifice merely because of some foolish words I said—" Linnea began when they were alone.

Everard put one gloved finger to her lips.

"Peace, Linnea. Your father is right. It is my duty to marry you, and I will do so gladly. You are owed a husband, and it is time I took a wife. In truth, I have conceived a great admiration for you. Will you accept me?"

A great admiration, indeed. Linnea knew he did not love her. How could he? She and her father had been nothing but a thorn in his side for weeks. If she accepted him, she knew the doyennes of society would be all atwitter when they learned about their hasty marriage and speculated on the cause of it. She was accustomed to being pilloried by the gossips, but how could she subject *him* to that?

He thought it was his duty to save her, of course. He was offering for her out of charity.

In addition to all his other familial burdens, Lord Stoke would assume responsibility for her father and end up paying the debts Lord Wrenthorpe would no doubt run up with the unlimited credit tradesmen were sure to grant him once he became the father-in-law of a very rich man.

Here was the man she had wanted since that day he came for her in Leicestershire, the most handsome, most honorable man in England. But if she truly cared for him, she told herself, she would refuse him.

He was, no matter how magnificently he was rising to the occasion, marrying her under duress. She *could* not accept this generosity from him.

Linnea opened her mouth to do the decent thing and refuse him, but the words would not come out.

Instead, she looked into his beautiful, earnest green eyes and was weak.

"Yes," she said, embarrassed by the way her voice quavered. "I will marry you."

He smiled at her, just as if she had made him the happiest of men, and raised her trembling hand to his lips.

Eleven

Linnea had accepted him.

She would be his in three weeks.

Everard grinned with giddy relief every time he thought about it, even though he knew the poor girl was desperate or she would have sent him about his business with one of those enchanting tirades that made her eyes glow and her delicate jaw lift with determination.

Eh, he had it bad. Very bad.

"You are looking remarkably cheerful for a fellow who has just possibly ruined his life," Michael said glumly as he joined him at the breakfast table. His face was mottled with temper. "Are you insane? The little shrew will have you under the cat's paw before the ink is dry on your marriage lines, and she'll be riding rough-shod over us all into the bargain. It is insufferable that you have put her in a position to queen it over Vittoria."

"As my wife, it will be her right."

"She will have little joy of it, I promise you," Michael said. "Do you think the whole world does not know you have agreed to marry her from pity because no one else will have her? Or that the members of your family are appalled by the match?"

Everard stood, grabbed Michael by the shirtfront, and yanked upward so he was forced to stand eye-to-eye with him. Since Michael was several inches shorter than Everard, he had to balance on his toes or choke.

"I cannot control what the gossips say," Everard said in

a low, menacing voice, "but the members of my own family will keep their mouths closed on the matter except to express their delight—their absolute *delight*—that Lady Linnea has done me the very great honor of consenting to be my wife. If anyone has the temerity to suggest that my feelings for Lady Linnea are anything but what they should be, or that Lady Linnea is unsuitable to be my wife, the members of my family will deny this emphatically. *Do* you understand?"

"I understand," Michael squeaked. "Completely."

Everard released his brother suddenly, and Michael had a brief, undignified struggle to remain upright.

"Has it occurred to you that it will be dashed awkward for Vittoria and me if Linnea comes to live here?" Michael said as he rubbed his throat as if to make sure it was still intact.

"When, not if," Everard said. "And you are absolutely right. It *will* be awkward. That is why you and Vittoria are going to have to find somewhere else to live. I should start looking at once, if I were you. Three weeks is not long to find a house to hire at the height of the Season."

Michael's mouth dropped open.

"You can't do this to us now. Vittoria is increasing."

"My congratulations," Everard said. "All the more reason for you to set up your own household."

"Very well," Michael said stiffly. "I will just instruct your secretary to seek out several suitable houses for Vittoria's approval and hire the one she chooses. I suppose your housekeeper can interview the servants on Vittoria's behalf. She is a bit of a slug-a-bed these days, poor pet."

"No, this transaction is nothing to do with me or my staff," Everard said deliberately. "*You* will find a suitable house, and you will pay for it, too."

"But—"

"Your means are ample for you to hire a modest house in town for the rest of the Season. If you find it so uncomfortable to remain in London for my wedding, then perhaps you would like to take yourself and your wife off to the country. I regret I cannot offer you the use of the dower house at my primary estate because it is occupied by our mother's cousins, but you can have a look at some of my minor unoccupied properties. Some are not in the best repair, but I am sure you and Vittoria will manage to make habitable whichever one you choose."

"How can you do this to your own flesh and blood?"

"I do nothing but make you responsible for the consequences of your own actions," Everard said. "You married Vittoria. You jilted Lady Linnea or, rather, you forced *me* to do it for you. Now you will support your wife decently on your bride's dowry and the allowance I will continue to make you."

"What about Elizabeth? Are you going to forget all about her memory now and marry another? I will tell you this: Linnea is no Elizabeth."

"No, she is not," Everard said. "And it is just as well. I am a grown man now with responsibilities, and I need a wife strong enough to shoulder them with me."

"It makes no sense, " Michael said, shaking his head in puzzlement. "You could have any woman you desire."

"And I will," Everard said quietly. "Understand this: Neither you nor your wife had better do *anything* to embarrass my future bride by your behavior or you will be sorry."

"You will cut off my allowance, I suppose," Michael said defiantly.

"Your very *generous* allowance," Everard reminded him. "Count on it."

With that, Michael huffed out of the room. The door had no sooner slammed than it was opened by a footman, and Lady Augusta sailed into the room, looking ready for battle.

Everard put his head in his hands.

"Everard!" Lady Augusta cried. "It will not do! A

wedding in three weeks? Are you *mad?* When you offered for Linnea, I had no idea you expected—"

"The nineteenth of June," Everard said, rising to tower
over her, "and not a day later. At St. Paul's, with a full choir
singing, a rose-festooned carriage waiting outside, as
many bridesmaids that may be gathered, and a wedding
breakfast for three hundred guests."

"Impossible!"

"Nonsense. Nothing is impossible for you, Aunt
Augusta."

His aunt was not impervious to this praise.

"Well, I am sure I can arrange *something*," she agreed
reluctantly. "But to do honor to the occasion in the time allowed will be a Herculean effort, and I warn you that it
will cost a pretty penny."

"I don't give a hang what it costs," he said.

Lady Augusta smiled beatifically at these magic words,
and Everard couldn't help smiling back at her.

"Excellent! I will not disappoint you," she said. He
could see the little wheels turning in her avaricious head.
Everard knew there was nothing she liked better than
throwing extravaganzas at Everard's expense. She gave
him a pretty pout. "But you must know it simply is not
done to send out invitations to a wedding only three weeks
before the date. Especially for the same date that the bride
originally intended to marry another man. Whether anyone who *is* anyone will come is another matter."

"Oh, they will come," Everard said sardonically. "To see
what foolish costume my future father-in-law will be
tricked out in for the occasion, if for no other reason."

"Well, the whole affair is most irregular," Lady Augusta
said with a delicate shudder. "What the gossips will make
of it, I can only imagine. It would make a much better appearance if we wait a few months. An autumn wedding
would be lovely."

"I have promised Linnea a husband by June 19, and that
is what she will have."

"But, still—"

"If any of the busybodies have the temerity to question it," he added ruefully, "you may tell them that I am eager to wed her at once for fear she will come to her senses and back out of the marriage."

"Back out of the marriage!" Augusta exclaimed. "Who would believe such a ridiculous faradiddle?"

"She is marrying me out of desperation, after all. You know very well she must marry *someone* to keep her father in line and pay off his remaining debts to the tradesmen."

"Nonsense! You do not know Linnea very well if you think she would marry anyone against her will."

"Well, she seemed perfectly willing to marry Lord Fleetwood and his demonic children or even the bald and toothless Lord Ormsley if either of them had come up to scratch, so that is nothing to puff myself up about."

"Oh, I think our Linnea is far from indifferent to your charms," she said shrewdly.

"She would not have entertained my suit for a moment if Whitcomb had possessed the bottom to stand up to his aunt."

"Whitcomb!" Augusta scoffed. "He's a very good-looking young man and closer to her in age, I'll give you that. But is he an earl? Does he own a mansion in Mayfair? Does he enjoy a position at the forefront of London society?"

"Linnea does not care about any of those things."

"No," Augusta said, "but she is very, very grateful to you for offering to marry her. She and her father would have been up the River Tick, if you had not. She would never renege on her promise to marry you now that she has made it."

"My point exactly," he said. "I am no substitute for the dashing young cavalry officer she expected to marry, but, by God, she *will* be able to hold her head up on her wedding day!"

"You may depend on me," Lady Augusta vowed with a gleam of pure pleasure at the prospect of being as extravagant as she chose in the matter of planning a wedding for her cherished goddaughter. "Now, about Linnea's gown. She intends to wear the same one she had made five years ago for her original wedding to Michael, and I am persuaded wearing it can only bring bad luck to the two of you."

"My wife is *not* going to be married in a gown she had made for her wedding to another man," Everard exclaimed. "Why would she even *consider* such a thing? I am not precisely a pauper!"

"She is embarrassed by the expense you must incur for this wedding, when it is the responsibility of her father to shoulder it instead, and she is determined to brush through the business as economically as possible."

"Laudable, but unnecessary," he said. "Lady Linnea's sense of honor is among her most admirable virtues, but I fear we must override her in this matter. My dignity and her own rank as the daughter of an earl demand it."

"And so I have told her," said Augusta triumphantly. "But I am afraid she is quite determined. She claims it is ridiculous to buy another—and pay the seamstress extra to make it up quickly—when this one has never been worn. I have talked to her until I am blue in the face, and she will not be swayed. Besides being sadly outmoded, the gown does not fit at all well because her figure has changed since she first came out of the schoolroom."

"You may leave the matter to me," he said, "and I thank you for bringing it to my attention.

With that, Lady Augusta smiled and took her leave, having achieved what she had set out to accomplish.

Linnea rose sleepily on one elbow and tossed her hair out of her eyes when an elegantly dressed, middle-aged woman sailed into her bedchamber with a small army of assistants trailing in her wake. Their arms were full of bolts of sumptuous fabrics and artificial flowers, and trimmings of lace and silver ribbon.

"Miss Lacey," Linnea gasped as she sat bolt upright and crossed her arms over the bosom of her night rail. "I am not dressed!"

"It is just as well, Lady Linnea," one of London's most exclusive seamstresses said purposefully. Her eyes were twinkling with enthusiasm and greed. "You only would have had to get undressed again, for I must take your measurements for your brideclothes. I thought white gauze and silver tissue with white silk roses for your wedding gown. Or did you have something else in mind?"

"I am afraid there has been some mistake," Linnea said. "I did not engage your services."

"No mistake," Miss Lacey said. "I am engaged to make your trousseau by your generous and handsome Lord Stoke, in the strictest confidence, of course." She made a coy little gesture of buttoning her lip. "I wish you every happiness, my dear young lady, as if that were at all in question! We must begin at once if we are to have everything completed in time.

"Such a *large* order," she added in pleased anticipation. "His lordship was quite specific about his requirements. What a fortunate young woman you are, if you will permit me to say so!"

Linnea thought she would die of shame.

She turned on Lady Augusta when she entered the room and stood regarding Linnea with a triumphant look on her face.

"You told him," Linnea said reproachfully. "Has he not given me enough already? Did I not say that I would not be obligated to Lord Stoke for the very clothes on my back on my wedding day?"

"I had to, love," Lady Augusta said, unrepentant. "Your old gown has a *train*. No one wears trains anymore."

Linnea gave a long sigh.

The gown not only had a demitrain, but also was festooned with a great many artificial violets, which, along with the once-pristine white muslin fabric, had not worn well in the years of the gown's careful storage in tissue.

She was perfectly aware that it had been designed for the romantic young girl of unsophisticated tastes she once had been, and was hardly appropriate for a woman of her age, but that was hardly to the point.

How could Linnea possibly justify accepting this exceedingly extravagant gift from a man to whom she already owed so much?

Miss Lacey stood at attention with her extremely well-trained assistants at the ready.

Linnea looked longingly at the lovely, forbidden fabrics—the silks, the satins, the elaborately patterned brocades and muslins and gauzes in every subtle shade of blindingly pristine white to elegant antique ivory—and faltered in her determination.

"Is it a just recompense for Everard's generosity to you, Linnea, for him to have to be ashamed of his bride's appearance on his wedding day?" Lady Augusta asked gently.

Linnea let all her breath out at once.

As justification, it would do perfectly well.

She would do it for *him*, of course. Not because the rigorously suppressed little imp that lived inside Linnea's heart and hungered for pretty things had broken free and was leaping for joy.

"You are right," she said, smiling at Miss Lacey, who sallied forth at once with her tape measure.

"I do not know how you will choose," Lady Augusta said happily as she indicated the bolts of fabric.

"That one," Linnea said without hesitation as she

pointed to the snowy white silk that had drawn her eye from the moment it had been brought into the room.

"An excellent choice," Miss Lacey said gleefully, by which Linnea knew she had chosen the most expensive fabric in the lot.

Twelve

Linnea's cheeks grew hot when she gazed upon the marquise-shaped sapphire in its gleaming platinum setting. It was glorious!

This was no dusty heirloom he had unearthed from the family vault. How had he known that she had thought the Stoke family betrothal ruby quite hideous on his mother's otherwise elegant hand when she was alive?

"I cannot," she gasped, wide-eyed with consternation as she took a step backward from the ice blue temptation in its presentation case of black velvet. They were in Lady Augusta's garden with the fairy glamour of fireflies all about them in the perfumed twilight. The jubilant imp in her heart was leaping for joy again. Linnea ruthlessly suppressed it. "No, Lord Stoke—"

"Everard," he said gently. He was so handsome and so earnest in his black evening kit and snowy white linen. She took an impetuous step back and turned away from him. His footsteps followed, and he was standing so close she could feel his breath on her hair. "My dear girl, what is this? You must have known that I would present you with a betrothal ring. I thought you would enjoy wearing it to the ball tonight."

"It is too much. I could not possibly accept—"

"Nonsense. What could be more appropriate for a bride whose eyes are to be compared with sapphires twinkling in the sunlight?" he asked with gentle mockery as he turned her around to face him and placed one hand under her chin to compel her to look at him.

She had to smile at that.

Then she sobered as she looked again at the gleaming gem. "It is enormous."

"So are your eyes right now."

She could only stare at him. She found it difficult to breathe as he closed his eyes and started to lean toward her. She closed her eyes as well and could not repress a sigh of anticipation.

Abruptly he stepped back, took her hand, and kissed the back of it.

Her eyes snapped open.

"That's done, then," he said briskly as he deftly took the ring and placed it on her finger.

"Thank you, Everard," she said. "It is the most beautiful thing I have ever seen."

Everard had to clamp his lips shut to keep from telling her that she was the most beautiful thing *he* had ever seen.

She was wearing the peach-colored silk brocade gown, the one that had almost caused him to swallow his tongue when he saw her in the library before Aunt Augusta's ball. A matching bandeau was entwined through her short, saucy dark curls.

He had almost lost his head and kissed her again. Thank God he had come to his senses in time.

Everard would not force her to endure his advances, even though her acceptance of his ring branded her as his.

Not until he knew she would welcome them.

A man had to have *some* pride.

"We must go," he said, steeling himself to leave the intimacy of the romantic twilight to escort her inside the house. "We do not want to be late for the ball on our first public appearance as a betrothed couple."

"Certainly not," she said in the same tone. "It would be *too déclassé* to make an entrance."

At that moment, a harassed Lady Augusta rushed to the doorway.

"Come quickly," she cried. "It's your father, Linnea."

"Father," Linnea repeated in alarm.

"He did not come home last night," Everard said as his heart clutched with foreboding.

"And you did not tell me?" she said.

"It was not the first time," he said defensively, knowing this would not absolve him from guilt if the worst had happened.

White-lipped, Linnea rushed past him and into the house as he dogged her heels.

"Papa," Linnea cried as she skidded into the room, fearing to find his lifeless body stretched out on a plank.

What she did see was every bit as shocking. She could feel Everard's arms grasp her shoulders protectively. It was either that, she supposed, or crash into her when she stopped so abruptly.

Lord Wrenthorpe was red-faced and breathless from the exertion of having borne a plump, blushing young woman dressed in the first stare of fashion over the threshold. She looked to be Linnea's age.

"Put me down," that female cried in high-pitched laughter. "You will do yourself an injury."

"Light as a feather, upon my word," he said cheerfully. Nevertheless, he carefully placed the stranger upon her own feet, with every appearance of relief.

"Papa?" Linnea said again as she held one hand over her racing heart.

"Linnea!" he said, just as if seeing her was an agreeable, but unexpected, surprise. "Here is your new daughter come to greet you," he said to his companion.

"Linnea, lovey," the woman said, grasping Linnea in her arms and giving her a hearty hug. Over her shoulder, Linnea gave her father a questioning look.

"Linnea," Lord Wrenthorpe said with a flourish, "I give you Lady Wrenthorpe, your new stepmother."

"Oh," Linnea said, taking the woman's shoulders and looking into her merry brown eyes. "I am . . . that is to say . . . welcome to the family."

"That's my girl," said her proud papa, beaming at the both of them. He seemed to notice a slack-jawed Everard for the first time. "Ah, Lord Stoke. Lady Wrenthorpe."

"A pleasure, my lady," Everard said, pulling himself together. "May I offer my felicitations?"

"Thank you, my lord," the new countess said, exchanging a look of pure mischief with her husband.

"Now you won't have to marry *him*," Lord Wrenthorpe said to Linnea, for all the world as if he were giving her good news.

"Not marry . . . Everard?" she faltered. She and Everard exchanged a look of pure perplexity.

"No need for it," her treacherous father said proudly. "You're off the hook, boy, because now that I've married Dora, I can take care of Linnea myself. Pack your things, girl. You're moving into our town house at once."

"Lord Wrenthorpe," said Everard.

"I haven't forgotten all the blunt you laid out for Linnea's furbelows," Lord Wrenthorpe said genially. "Give me a Dutch reckoning, and I'll settle it with you tomorrow."

"I don't give a hang for that," Everard said, "but I have not withdrawn my suit for Linnea's hand, nor do I intend to. The announcement has already gone to the newspapers."

"The betrothal won't be announced in the papers," Lord Wrenthorpe said. "I stopped by the newspaper offices myself to withdraw the announcement before it could be published. Run along, Linnea. It was a long journey from Scotland, and we have much to do."

Lady Augusta, who was uncharacteristically mute up to now, stepped forward to perform her duties as hostess.

"Lady Wrenthorpe," she said, "will you be seated? I will ring for refreshments."

"Thank you," the lady said with a grin. She had flaming

red hair and freckles that competed with her vibrant green traveling costume for attention.

"I know who you are!" Lady Augusta said suddenly. "Miss Dora Watson, who married Mr. Timmons."

Augusta normally didn't pay attention to gossip about her social inferiors, but London was abuzz when this girl of good family had been virtually sold at a criminally young age to an elderly tradesman by her greedy relatives. No one had seen her in years, although Mr. Timmons's death announcement had appeared in the newspapers some months ago. The old man had been known as a greedy, avaricious old scoundrel who was so jealous of his young wife that he kept her a virtual prisoner in her own home. Ironically, Mr. Timmons was one of Lord Wrenthorpe's most persistent creditors. The woman had experienced little kindness in her life. No wonder she had succumbed to Lord Wrenthorpe's cheerful good humor. The only kind thing her former husband had done for her was die and leave her the only heir to his fortune.

"You have a good memory, Lady Augusta," the countess said, looking self-conscious. She turned to look at her new husband. "Marrying Lord Wrenthorpe is the best thing that ever happened to me," she said earnestly. "I have always wanted to be a grand lady and have a handle to my name. I will do everything in my power to make him happy."

Lord Wrenthorpe kissed his wife's hand.

"You already have, my love," he murmured with a wicked smile that made his wife blush crimson.

"You old goat!" Lady Augusta exclaimed with pure loathing. "How *could* you take advantage of the poor little thing?"

Lady Wrenthorpe shot to her feet, ready to do battle.

"Steady, there, Dora," her laughing husband said, springing up and catching her by her shoulders, presumably so she wouldn't plant her hostess a facer. "She's right, you know. I don't half deserve you."

"I don't half deserve *you*," the doting wife said lovingly.
Lady Augusta rolled her eyes.

Before she could say anything, Linnea reappeared with
her maid carrying two bandboxes, and two footmen carrying her trunks. She had exchanged her ball gown for a
traveling costume.

Everard started forward, but Linnea averted her face and
walked past him.

"Linnea," he called after her. "We must talk."

"You can call on Linnea at our town house tomorrow,"
Lord Wrenthorpe said smugly, and ushered his women out
the door with the maid and footmen following.

"Whoever would have thought it?" Lady Augusta said,
practically falling into a chair when they were gone. "The
old goat *did* find himself a rich wife, after all."

"How rich is she?" Everard asked. It was hard to make
his lips move. He was still in shock.

"Enormously," Lady Augusta said in awe. "Fabulously.
She has almost as much money as you do. Linnea's disgusting father can buy her a marquess, if she has a fancy
to have one."

She gave a long sigh and smiled ruefully at Everard.

"Well, he is right about one thing. There is definitely no
need for you and Linnea to marry. Fortunately, the invitations have not yet gone to the post. I suppose you are in no
humor to attend the ball, after all?"

And have everyone stare at him, the way they had stared
at Linnea when Michael jilted her?

"No," he said grimly. "I must rise early in the morning."

He planned to be on Linnea's doorstep far in advance of
proper calling hours.

Linnea regarded the boyishly handsome man kneeling
romantically before her chair with growing cynicism.

It certainly had not taken Mr. Whitcomb long to learn

that her father had married Mr. Timmons's widow along with the late tradesman's fabulous fortune.

"I could not stay away an instant longer," he declared passionately. "Your face was before me every moment."

By this, Linnea supposed, he meant that his aunt had withdrawn her opposition to the match.

"Mr. Whitcomb, stand up," she said in a no-nonsense voice. "I cannot marry you."

"I know what it is," he said. "You feel obligated to Stoke. But he is too old and sober for a lively woman of spirit such as yourself. A good man in his way—"

"And worth ten of you. Stand up, sir. At once," she said.

Instead, he rose and trapped her within the arms of her chair by placing his hands on them.

He leaned forward and kissed her. When he did, she drew back, dealt him a ringing slap, and scrubbed her lips with one hand.

"Get *off*," she snapped.

"Why, you little—" he began as he grasped her shoulders.

"You heard the lady," said a quiet voice from behind him.

Mr. Whitcomb straightened up and turned to face Everard.

He flushed scarlet.

"I think you should go," Everard said with a straight face. "Or I won't lift a finger to save you from having your claret drawn."

With an exclamation of annoyance, Mr. Whitcomb walked around Everard and stomped out of the room.

"*That*," said Linnea in disgust, "has been going on all morning. What has taken you so long?"

"Well, I . . . what do you mean?"

"There," she said, wresting the sapphire ring off her finger and handing it to him. "Did you think I did not know you would make haste to withdraw your suit now that you no longer feel honor-bound to marry me?"

"It was a match that you accepted in desperation."

"Oh, by all means act the martyr," she snapped, "just as if you were not jumping for joy at your narrow escape."

"I am doing nothing of the kind," he said, annoyed. "You certainly will not lack for suitors if I withdraw from the lists."

"Fortune hunters, every one," she said. "When I was poor, I didn't have all of your greedy friends underfoot, petitioning for my hand. At least *you* did not want to marry me for my money. *Damn* you, Everard."

"Linnea!" he exclaimed, shocked, not only by the unladylike profanity but also by the sheen of tears that gleamed in her eyes. He put his hands on her shoulders. "What is this? You should be happy. You can marry anyone you want."

"Don't you see that is impossible, because *you* are the one I want?" she snapped. Her face was flushed with temper, her eyes were narrowed to slits, and her nose was red from her efforts to stop from crying as she uttered this loverlike sentiment.

Instead of enfolding her in his arms as he ardently wished to do, however, he could not help laughing for sheer, exuberant joy.

"Don't you *dare* laugh at me," she said, poking him in the chest with her forefinger. Still laughing, he retreated as she advanced, backing him right up against the wall.

"I'm not laughing at you, sweetheart," he said. "I'm laughing at myself for being such a fool. I thought you were marrying *me* for my money."

A smile burst upon Linnea's face as bright as the sun. She threw her arms around his neck and raised her face for his kiss. Possessively, he placed his hands on her waist and fairly drooled with anticipation as he contemplated her closed eyelids and flushed cheeks.

Then he muttered a curse and drew back.

"What is wrong now?" she asked, opening her eyes and staring at him in consternation as he dropped to his knees.

"I dropped the bloody ring," he said, goaded beyond endurance.

"Oh, no!" she wailed as she plopped down on the carpet beside him.

Much to the detriment of her pretty yellow muslin gown, she stretched almost full length on the floor and poked her head under a chair to feel the carpeting with her searching fingers.

He grasped her waist and drew her out, enjoying a glimpse of slim ankle from beneath her jumbled skirts as he did so.

"Never mind, love," he said, just before he kissed her. "I'll buy you another."

They reluctantly broke apart when they heard a startled exclamation torn from a male throat, and Everard rolled to his side to regard his erstwhile friend, the cavalry officer, with a bouquet of spring flowers in his hand.

"You're too late," Linnea snarled fiercely. "Go *away*!"

Thirteen

"She never looked at *me* like that," Michael whispered pettishly to his wife as the slim, lovely new Countess of Stoke practically devoured her bridegroom with her dark blue eyes at the altar of St. Paul's, just after the bishop had pronounced them man and wife. She was wearing an elegant gown in white silk that fit her like a second skin. Her veil was suspended from a diamond tiara, and she carried a stunning bouquet of white orchids tied in silver ribbon.

Every once in a while she would glance down at her sapphire betrothal ring as if she were checking to make sure it was still there.

After an exhaustive search by practically everyone in her father's household, the ring had been found under a table. Everard had made a very funny story of it last night at dinner.

"I will scratch her eyes out," purred Vittoria as she looked down ruefully at her own rounded figure. Her pregnancy was not far advanced, but she had been queasy in the mornings and her gowns were uncomfortably snug through the waistline these days.

Michael's heart turned over, and he kissed her hand, even though he knew the probable cause of his wife's envy was Linnea's slender figure and not her prior claim on Michael himself.

"No need, love," Michael said. "I wish my poor brother joy of her. Indeed, he has my deepest sympathy."

Unaware that he was to be pitied, Everard escorted his

bride to the flower-festooned carriage to lead the procession to her father's town house for the wedding breakfast. Applause broke out from the crowd that had gathered outside the church to see the bride's gown and observe who among the nobs saw fit to attend the ceremony.

"Look at me, the toast of society," she joked to Everard as she graciously acknowledged the applause.

"Yes. Look at you," he said, amused by her simple pleasure at the attention.

He assisted her into the carriage.

"It would be an *open* carriage," he complained into her ear. "I don't know how much longer I can wait to get you alone. Would it be unforgivable of us to forego the wedding breakfast?"

"But I'm *starving*!" she said soulfully.

"So am I," he said in a tone of voice that made her cheeks flame with color.

Historical Romance from
Jo Ann Ferguson

Discover the Thrill of
Romance With
Lisa Plumley

__Making Over Mike__

0-8217-7110-8   **$5.99US/$7.99CAN**

Amanda Connor is a life coach—not a magician! Granted, as a televised publicity stunt for her new business, the savvy entrepreneur has promised to transform some poor slob into a perfectly balanced example of modern manhood. But Mike Cavaco gives "raw material" new meaning. With her future at stake, what can Amanda do but roll up her sleeves, get down to work . . . and pray for a miracle?

__Falling for April__

0-8217-7111-6   **$5.99US/$7.99CAN**

Her hometown gourmet catering company may be in a slump, but April Finnegan isn't about to begin again. Determined to save her business, she sets out to win some local sponsors, unaware she's not the only one in Saguaro Vista with that idea. Turns out wealthy department store mogul Ryan Forrester is one step—and thousands of dollars—ahead of her. Clearly, this sunny southwestern town isn't big enough for both of them. Somebody has to go— and it sure isn't going to be April!
